A GOOD MULE
is HARD
to FIND

A GOOD MULE
is HARD
to FIND

and other tales from red clay country

Kirk H. Neely

Emory Cash, Illustrator

Spartanburg • 2009

First printing, October 2009
Second printing, November 2009
Third Printing, October 2010

Hub City editor: Jeremy L.C. Jones
Copy editors: Carol Bradof, Betsy Wakefield Teter, Winnie Walsh, Jameelah Lang
Book design: Mark Olencki
Illustrations: Emory Cash
Front, back, and title page photographs: Mark Olencki
Printed by McNaughton & Gunn, Saline, MI

Library of Congress Cataloging-in-Publication Data

Neely, Kirk H.
  A good mule is hard to find / Kirk H. Neely.
    p. cm.
  ISBN 978-1-891885-67-9 (pbk.)
  1. Neely, Kirk H.—Childhood and youth—Anecdotes. 2. Spartanburg County (S.C.)—
Social life and customs—20th century—Anecdotes. 3. Country life—South Carolina—
Spartanburg County—Anecdotes. 4. Neely, Kirk H.—Anecdotes. I. Title.
  F277.S7N44 2009
  975.7'29043—dc22

                              2009027925

Hub City Writers Project
PO Box 8421
Spartanburg SC 29305
(864) 577-9349 • www.hubcity.org

Dedicated to my dad, the original Kirk Neely

*The Hub City Writers Project thanks the following
who helped underwrite publication of this book:*

Mr. and Mrs. Robert Caldwell
Dr. and Mrs. Paul Cook
Mr. and Mrs. Dave Edwards
Mr. and Mrs. John Faris
Mrs. Harry Gibson
Dr. and Mrs. Bob Haas
Dr. and Mrs. Hugh Hayes
Mr. and Mrs. Jim Joyner
Mr. and Mrs. Ken Neely
Mr. and Mrs. Kirk Neely Sr.
Mr. and Mrs. Robert Pinson

TABLE OF CONTENTS

Introduction: *Storytelling Is in My Blood*

"I remember running naked through the woods with you," my pharmacist said to me recently. The other customers in Smith's Drug Store #2 shot strange looks at both of us, my old friend and me.

Perish the thought of these two sixty-something-year-old men running through the woods at all, much less without proper attire!

Actually my friend was exaggerating. At the time of our woodland escapades we were Boy Scouts scantily clad in what we thought was authentic Cherokee Indian regalia. The Native Americans who inhabited the forest long before our romp would have been far more discreet.

"I also remember sitting around a campfire listening to you spin those yarns," he said. "You know, Kirk, even back then you were a storyteller. Every boy in the troop loved to hear your tall tales."

Years later, on the plains of Indiana, I received a similar affirmation from Abe Conklin, then the Headman of the Ponca people of Oklahoma.

Fanning smoke of smoldering cedar and sage over me with the wing of a golden eagle, Abe acknowledged my role as a pastor and my responsibilities as husband, father, and uncle. He said, "You are a weaver of words, a keeper of wisdom."

Storytelling is a treasured part of my heritage. My grandfather had a tale suitable for every occasion.

I have dedicated this book to my dad. Now in his eighty-eighth year, Dad is a master storyteller. My earliest memory of a religious experience is of Dad telling the Old Testament account of Gideon, the man who won without fighting.

My uncles on both sides of the family have been repositories of treasured family memories preserved through oral tradition.

My father-in-law, Mr. Jack, was a delightful storyteller. As was often my experience with my grandfather and my dad, Mr. Jack and I could exchange tales for hours at mealtimes.

Lest I err by implying that storytelling is only a male endeavor, let me be quick to add that my mother and my grandmothers shared their own wisdom through stories, usually read out loud. It is one of the reasons that I value books as I do.

Every generation has asked, "Why is storytelling so important?"

My best answer is to tell a story.

Creech spent most afternoons sitting on the front porch of his Barnwell County farmhouse. Children of all ages enjoyed stopping by for a visit. The old man always had a tale or two to tell.

"Uncle Creech, why do you tell so many stories?" his nephew asked.

"I'll be glad to explain, but would you bring me some cool water first?"

The boy walked across the yard to the well. He lowered the wooden bucket to the bottom of the shaft and cranked it back up to the top of the well. He filled a gourd dipper from the bucket and carried it to his uncle.

"Thank you, kindly," old man Creech said. "The water is mighty good, but why did you bring me the dipper when I only asked for water?"

"How could I bring you water without something to hold it?"

"And that is exactly why I tell these tales. Stories hold the truth I want to give to you."

Stories are the vessels in which wisdom is contained. Aesop told fables, Jesus told parables, and the best teachers have followed their examples. Stories are the containers into which moral instruction, deep pathos, and real humor are poured.

I am sometimes asked, "Where do you get all of your stories?" For me, it is a matter of paying attention. I find stories everywhere, in everything I read, in every conversation, in silent encounters during the course of every day. Every person has a story to tell. He or she is almost always willing to tell it if someone is willing to take the time to listen.

"How do you remember so many stories?"

Stories have great potential but a very short life expectancy. They have to be used quickly or stored for later.

One way to remember is to keep a journal. I almost always have a notebook and pen close at hand. Another way to remember is to tell the story to another person soon after you hear it. Every time you tell it, the story becomes more deeply implanted in your own mind.

"Are these stories true?"

All stories tell the truth, even those that are fiction. In the best storytelling tradition, the truth is far more important than fact. In fact, fiction is one of the best ways to tell the truth.

Storytelling, like story writing, rings true when it is about what you know and where you live. Ernest Hemingway wrote one of my favorites: *The Old Man and the Sea*. He understood the power of a blue marlin. Mark Twain wrote the definitive American novel about life on the Mississippi River where he grew up.

These stories are about my neck of the woods. Just like my blue jeans after an adventure in Dead Horse Canyon, these tales are caked with red clay. They are from the Blue Ridge Mountains, from the rivers of the Piedmont, from the cotton mills, and from the lumberyard.

After our nine-year-old son had spun a long yarn in his third-grade class, the teacher asked, "Where did you hear that story?"

"My dad told it to me," he said.

"And did your father teach you to tell stories?" the teacher inquired.

"No, ma'am. It just runs in our family."

Each week for the last four years I have written "By The Way," a column for *HJ Weekly*. I write about the ordinary—casseroles and sweet tea, black bears and beagle dogs, WD-40 and duct tape, Tabasco sauce and fatback. *A Good Mule Is Hard to Find* is a collection of fifty of those columns. The striking pen and ink sketches by my nephew, Emory Cash, highlight each piece.

These stories are rooted and grounded in the South. Some will make you laugh out loud; others will bring a tear to your eye. All are memorable.

Some of these stories will comfort you like soul food. Others will be as refreshing as a tall glass of sweet iced tea. A few are spicy like Tabasco sauce. My hope is that they will inspire you to tell a story or two about where you live and the people you know.

Spray a little WD-40 on your rocking chair, kick back, and enjoy!

—Kirk H. Neely
March 2009

A Good Mule is Hard to Find

Dick spent most of his life working on the chain gang. In 1930 during the Great Depression, my grandfather Pappy bought him at auction for fifteen dollars. Dick was a mule that had been used and abused until he was little more than skin and bones. He had been in harness so many times that the trace chains had rubbed open sores on his sides.

Pappy got a jar of Bluestone Salve to put on the mule's sores. He fed him oats, corn, and hay to put a little meat on his bones. When Dick was restored to health, he was an excellent plow mule.

Though good at plowing, Dick never liked to be ridden. If a person tried to mount him like a horse, the mule would kick and bite.

My dad and his brothers would lead Dick underneath a Chinaberry tree. They'd drop a pillow on his back to get him used to carrying a little weight. Then, from a limb above, they would ease onto the mule so they could ride him. If they rode him down to the highway, Dick would balk, refusing to go out into the road. All those years on the chain gang made him leery.

A mule is a cross between a donkey and a horse. A mule may be a male or a female. Both are sterile. They cannot reproduce. A mule's ears are long and turn toward to the slightest sound. Mules have a unique voice that is a combination of a horse's whinny and a donkey's bray.

During the Great Depression, many a dirt farmer depended on a mule. In fact, having a mule was better than having a horse. Paul and Betsy Hutchins, founders of the American Donkey and Mule Society and co-authors of *The Modern Mule*, explain:

• Mules endure heat better than horses. They drink only enough water to replace lost body fluids.

• Mules consume less food than horses. They rarely overeat.

• Mules are sure-footed. Their hooves are strong and flexible, while horses are prone to hoof problems.

• Mules are physically strong and live longer productive years than horses.

• Mules require less veterinary care than horses.

• Mules are not inclined to panic.

• Mules have a strong sense of self-preservation. If they are overheated, overworked, or overused, mules will either slow down or stop. They are not stubborn, but they will not put themselves in danger.

• Mules are intelligent animals. They respond well to a firm, gentle hand.

Pappy used to tell the story about a farmer who was left in dire straits after his mule died. He was having trouble making ends meet. He tried to cut corners every way that he could. He owned no farm equipment other than a mule and a plow. The mule, Humphrey, was a fine, strong animal, essential to the making and harvesting of crops.

One of the farmer's cost-saving measures was to mix a little sawdust into the oats that he fed Humphrey. At first it seemed to be a workable plan. When he told his neighbors about it, they thought it an odd way to take care of a good mule, but Humphrey seemed to hold up.

The months passed and times got worse. The farmer mixed more sawdust with the oats he fed Humphrey. The mule grew weaker but still worked as hard as he could.

One day a neighbor asked, "How are things going?"

"Not good. Not good at all. Just about the time I got Humphrey on all sawdust and no oats, that mule up and died."

Humphrey died just before spring planting. The farmer had to buy another mule. He scraped together thirty dollars. He couldn't buy a mule as good as Humphrey, but he was satisfied with the animal. At Cudd's Mule Barn he made arrangements to return the next day with a borrowed truck to pick up the mule. The dealer agreed to keep the animal overnight.

When the farmer returned, he was greeted with more bad news.

The mule dealer said, "I'm real sorry to have to tell you this. I know you were countin' on that mule for your spring planting, but he died last night."

The dealer didn't offer to refund his money because a deal was a deal. The farmer loaded the dead mule on the truck and left.

A couple of months later, the mule dealer happened to drive by the farmer's place. He was astonished to see him working his garden on a Ford tractor. He called the farmer over to ask how in the world he had managed to buy a tractor when, not too long ago, all he had was thirty dollars to spend on the dead mule.

"Well," the farmer explained, "after leaving with the dead mule,

I stopped off at the local print shop. I had some two-dollar raffle tickets printed up to say, 'Grand Prize: Used Gardening Equipment.' I sold the raffle tickets to people around town."

"Okay, but where did you get the gardening equipment?"

"From you."

"But all you got from me was a dead mule."

"I know. That's what I raffled off."

"You raffled off a dead mule? I'll bet it really ticked 'em off when they realized the mule was dead."

"Nope. Not really. The only one that got mad was the winner, and I gave him his two dollars back."

A Lumberyard Education

My grandfather was born in Tennessee in 1889. I called him Pappy. He dropped out of school in the eighth grade to support his mother and three siblings following the death of his father in a railroad accident. Enlisting in the United States Navy at age nineteen, Pappy served four years in Cuba. Upon his discharge, he worked for a telegraph company as a lineman. His company sent him to the Lowcountry of South Carolina to do the electrical wiring for a sawmill. At a cake walk at the Methodist church in Estill, he met the woman who would become his wife and my grandmother, Mammy.

In 1925, Pappy and Mammy moved to Spartanburg where he opened his own lumberyard.

During the Great Depression, they lost everything. With grit and faith, they raised nine children, sweet potatoes, and turkeys on a rented red clay farm in Cedar Springs. Following the Depression, Pappy opened another lumberyard, a family business still in operation today.

When I was a boy, I wanted to work at the lumberyard when I grew up. It was a natural thing. The men that I admired most worked at the lumberyard: Dad and Pappy. My dad told me I could have a job, but he said, "Before you work at the lumberyard, you have to learn to work for your mama."

Working for my mother was harder than working anywhere else. Finally, I got the promotion! I went to work at the lumberyard the summer after I finished the seventh grade. I weighed no more than a 120 pounds soaking wet.

The very first day on the job, my dad put me to the task of unloading a boxcar of cement. The old boxcar had just one door. In those days, nothing was palletized. Forklifts were not yet available. All the cement had to be taken out by hand—one ninety-six-pound bag at a time—put on hand trucks, rolled up a ramp, and loaded into a warehouse. Fortunately, my dad knew that I did not need to work by myself. The man who worked

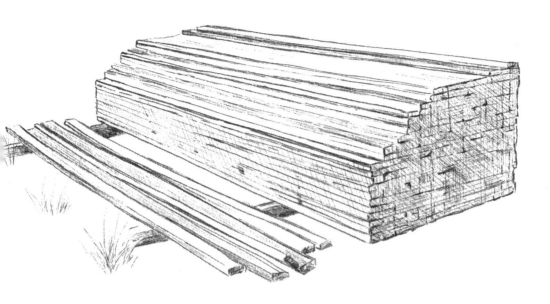

with me was Charlie Norman.

I don't know how old Charlie was when I started working with him. I asked him one time. He said he was as old as dirt. I didn't ask again, but I knew Charlie was very old. He had been working for my grandfather since before the Depression, delivering lumber in a one-horse wagon.

I will never forget that first day on the job working with Charlie. Those bags of cement were nearly a hundred pounds of dead weight. Charlie would stack them eight and nine high on the hand trucks, break the hand trucks down, and roll them up the ramp. I could put no more than three bags on the hand trucks. I had to jump up and put all my weight on the handles to break it down. It was all I could do to roll the hand trucks up the ramp. Most of the time, I had to turn around backwards and pull the load up the ramp.

By about 10 a.m., I was drenched with sweat and covered with sticky cement. Charlie peeled off his shirt. His ebony skin glistened. He looked like a bodybuilder. He was an old man whose muscles were toned by hard work.

We took a half-hour break for lunch, not nearly enough time for me. I was determined to work as hard as Charlie did. About 3 p.m., Charlie got his second wind. He started whistling in a low whisper of a whistle. By 4 p.m., he was singing. We had worked all day long. I was bone tired. Charlie was singing a low song under his breath. "We'll work till Jesus comes. We'll work till Jesus comes, and we'll be carried home."

Toward the end of the day, that song became a part of his work. It became almost a chant, a mantra. He sang, and he sang, and he sang.

When Dad and I got home, I took a shower. Mama had fixed a special meal, fried chicken, rice and gravy. I went to sleep at the supper table. Dad took me to my bed, tucked me in, had a prayer with me, and woke me at 5 a.m. for my second day of work. Charlie was already there when Dad and I arrived. I worked all summer long, earning the grand sum of two dollars a day.

I learned a lot that summer. I asked my Dad years later why he started me with such a difficult job.

"I wanted you to learn that this is hard work. Money doesn't grow on trees even after they've been sawed into lumber."

I asked why he paid me so little.

He grinned, "Be glad I didn't pay you what you were worth."

I learned to drive that summer—a three-ton lumber truck. Of course, I didn't drive on the highway, just around the stacks of lumber.

I learned that work is a noble endeavor.

As much as I enjoyed working with men I admired, as much as I enjoyed talking with customers, I didn't have to work at a lumberyard very long before I heard the Lord calling me to do something else.

How to Get Rid of a Possum

Few of us welcome untamed creatures in or around our homes. My wife, Clare, and I have had a number of close encounters of the wild kind at our house. While our exterminator faithfully deals with the usual roaches, ants, wasps, and mice, we have also hosted squirrels, snakes, bats, and owls as uninvited visitors.

Our sweet daughter-in-law, Patrice, phoned me one weekend with concern in her voice. "Papa Kirk, can you please tell me how I can get rid of a possum!"

"Why do you want to get rid of him?" I inquired.

"Because he's ugly and scary, and I don't like for him to be under my deck!"

Patrice is right. A possum is an undesirable houseguest.

Most of us consider possums to be annoying varmints. Opossums, to use the proper name, are our only native North American marsupial. They are first cousins to the Australian kangaroo. Females have a pouch on their belly where the young, up to thirteen in number, are carried and nourished for about two months after birth.

Adult possums can be three feet long, including the prehensile tail. They can hang from a tree limb, a posture immortalized by the character in the comic strip *Pogo*.

They weigh as much as fourteen pounds depending on how well-fed they are. Possums are omnivores. That means they will eat anything. Their diet includes insects, snails, rodents, berries, fruit, grasses, and leaves. Possum favorites seem to be pet food, garbage, and other roadkill. Yum! They are nocturnal animals, prowling around at night and sleeping during the day.

Playing possum is a defensive tactic the critter employs when frightened. Playing possum is feigning death. If you see one lying in the middle of the road, he is probably not pretending. Chances are he is really dead.

When I was a boy, my family lived on a dirt road until the area across the road from us was developed and homes were built. Early one morning, construction workers across the way found a possum scuffling around inside a nail keg where garbage had been thrown the day before. They trapped the possum by putting a scrap of hardware cloth over the keg, holding it in place with a brick.

I wandered across the road to see what was going on, and they said I could have the possum for a pet. Wow! That afternoon, my dad and I built a cage that looked something like a rabbit pen. My pet possum had a home, or so I thought. The next morning I found the cage empty. The possum had chewed through the wood. Blood was everywhere, and the possum was gone. Possums don't make good pets.

Possums are not clean animals. They can carry parasites and rabies, although rabies incidents are less frequent than in other animals, such as raccoons. Possums have strong immune systems. Possums also have a strong offensive odor, except to other possums. That is the reason they have so many little possums.

Because possums are prolific, they often have to find new places to live. They will live in a variety of habitats. They will make themselves right at home when they move into the neighborhood. Undersides of porches, decks, and tool sheds provide an ideal home. That puts them within striking distance to raid garbage cans and steal pet food. They are excellent climbers. Possums can be found living in attics, where they make a terrible mess and a lot of noise. It is a very good idea to get rid of possums if they are hanging out around your house.

Have you ever wondered how to get rid of a possum? There is no magic spray or device to make them go away. Some people have tried predator urine, such as coyote or fox urine, to get rid of possums. Not only does it not keep possums away, it makes the odor problem worse, and it is hard to come by. Coyotes and foxes are not necessarily interested in cooperating.

Some have recommended mothballs or ammonia-soaked rags to make possums leave, but that doesn't always work either. One way to take care of the possum problem is by trapping and removing them.

My sister-in-law tells about a time when a couple in her church in rural North Carolina paid a visit to her home. The woman had long gray hair. It was pulled up into a large 1970s-style beehive hairdo held in place by maximum-strength hair spray. In the course of the conversation, my sister-in-law thought she saw something moving in the woman's hair. Struggling to maintain eye contact, my sister-in-law again caught a glimpse of a small face peeking out from the beehive. She politely asked about the critter in the hairdo. The woman pulled three baby possums out of her elaborate hairdo, and, turning to her husband, said, "Show 'er the ones you've got, Earl." Earl reached into his shirt and brought from his considerable chest hair another two baby possums.

"Ain't they cute? Their mama got killed in the road in front of our place, so we took 'em in," the woman explained.

My sister-in-law was speechless for a moment and then recovered, "What are you going to do with them?"

"We're gonna keep 'em and fatten 'em up. Then we're gonna eat 'em."

That's one way to get rid of a possum.

A Bird with a Broken Wing

I sat with my friend Frank Nantz in a hospital room shortly before his death. He asked me to write this story for him.

I wish you, the reader, could have heard Frank narrate this account in person. His Chesnee accent, his unique dialect, made the telling far more delightful than I can ever achieve through the printed word. I relate the story in the first person, as if Frank were telling it.

*****

I worked for Foremost Dairies over twenty-one years. I started out driving a milk truck. Later, I was promoted to supervisor and then to sales manager. Eventually, the company decided to send me to be a plant manager in Sylacauga, Alabama. I explained that I didn't want to go to Sylacauga, Alabama, or to anywhere else. I wanted to stay in Spartanburg County.

My wife, our two daughters, my mother and father, my mother-in-law and father-in-law didn't want us to leave. I had fifty head of cattle on my farm in the northern end of the county. My cattle didn't want me to leave either.

When I told my company I wasn't going to Sylacauga, Alabama, I was offered more money. I assured them that it wouldn't be enough to get me to move. Because I refused to relocate, Foremost Dairies sent me to Jacksonville, Florida, for an evaluation. I met with Melvin Reid, Ph.D., for the better part of an afternoon. His office was on the top floor of the Gulf Life Building.

Dr. Reid gave me a test that asked five hundred of the silliest questions I have ever heard in all my life. Do you vomit at the sight of blood? Do dirty hands make you sick? Would you rather be an airplane pilot or a coal miner? Do you love your father more than your mother?

I did well on many of the questions about current events. I read a lot, and I enjoyed answering those questions. Some of the questions were just plain ridiculous.

Question Number 178 asked: If you found a bird with a broken wing, would it make you sad? I studied that question a few moments. I decided to leave it blank.

I finished the test. Dr. Reid looked over my answers, then slid his glasses down to the end of his nose like an old maid schoolteacher.

"Mr. Nantz, you didn't answer Question Number 178."

I explained that Question Number 178 did not give enough information.

Dr. Reid looked down at his notes for several minutes. He read the question aloud, "If you found a bird with a broken wing, would it make you sad?"

He asked, "Mr. Nantz, how much more information do you need?"

"I need to know what kind of bird you're asking me about."

"Mr. Nantz, please tell me why it matters what kind of bird has a broken wing?"

I answered, "Dr. Reid, you've been cooped up in this big Gulf Life Building too long. You need to get out more."

Dr. Reid slid those little glasses back down to the end of his nose. "Mr. Nantz, I want to hear your explanation. I've got all afternoon."

Sitting with Dr. Reid at the top of the Gulf Life Building, I explained:

"Travel east on Cannon's Campground Road in Spartanburg County, you will see bluebird boxes, some on fence posts, some on telephone poles. Turn left on Highway 110, near Cowpens. Continue to the county line. You will arrive at my farm. All along that stretch of road, I have put up bluebird boxes that I have built. I clean them out each winter and keep them fixed up each year. I refer to that road as the Frank Nantz Bluebird Trail.

"Dr. Reid, if I was walking my bluebird trail and found a little bluebird with a broken wing, I would pick that bird up in my hands. It would break my heart. I might even cry.

"Now, Dr. Reid, I have a bird dog, a fine pointer named Tonya. I love to go quail hunting. Tonya can flush a covey of quail better than any dog I have seen. With my pump shotgun, I have hit as many as five quail in one covey on the rise.

"Dr. Reid, my bird dog and I will ramble through bramble briars and blackberry vines until we find those quail. I take those little dead birds and put them in the pocket of my hunting jacket. If one of those quail is still alive but has a broken wing, I wring her neck and put her into that big pocket in my jacket with the others.

"Dr. Reid, I don't feel one bit sad about that because those quail will soon be my supper."

****

In his evaluation of Frank Nantz, Dr. Reid was complimentary. His recommendation to Foremost Dairies regarding Frank:

"Do not let this man leave your company. Do not send him to Sylacauga, Alabama. Let him stay in Spartanburg County. His wife, his two daughters, his parents, his in-laws, and fifty head of cattle all want him to stay. And while a few quail might like to see him leave, many more bluebirds want him to stay right where he is."

A Funny Thing Happened on the Way to the Cemetery

Every mortician and every pastor knows that funerals are fraught with opportunities for mistakes. A funeral is a somber time, a time to attend to the needs of the bereaved, a time to be serious, reverent, and, well, funereal. Still, the final service for a dearly departed loved one can be the occasion for humor.

The late Reverend Grady Nutt, a friend from my seminary days, was dubbed by the television program "Hee-Haw" as the Prime Minister of Humor. Grady was a master storyteller whose favorite targets were men of the cloth. He told the story about a young pastor who conducted his first graveside funeral during a Texas rainstorm. Things went pretty well in spite of the steady downpour until the closing prayer. The novice minister was speaking loudly to the Almighty when he suddenly fell silent. After a few moments, some of the gathered faithful cautiously opened their eyes. The young cleric had vanished from sight. It seems he stepped too close to the muddy grave and slid feet first under the suspended casket into the vault below.

Even a seasoned pastor can make embarrassing mistakes at funerals. A dear friend and colleague had to do two funerals in the same day, each for a fine man in his congregation. One of the deceased had been an outstanding high school and college athlete who spent most of his life as a coach. The other had been a more reticent, studious young man who had become successful in the financial world. The first was an avid sports fan; the second had little interest in sports. In the second funeral of the day, my colleague started eulogizing the wrong man. He spoke about the athletic prowess of a man who had never participated in organized sports. When the pastor caught himself, he apologized and added, "He always wished he could have been a great athlete."

A recent seminary graduate, newly ordained, accepted his first pastorate in a rural area in northern Spartanburg County. Soon after his arrival at the church, he was asked to conduct a funeral for an elderly man. The man was a longtime member of the church but had been unable to attend services in several years because of ill health. The family explained that the funeral service was to be graveside at the family cemetery located at the old home place in southern Union County. The service was to be brief and would be followed by a covered dish dinner provided by the good folks at a nearby church.

The young pastor was nervous as he prepared for his first funeral. He rehearsed the service in his mind as he followed a set of complicated directions to the remote home. He became hopelessly lost on the back roads of Union County near Sumter National Forest. Finally, almost by accident, he came upon the old house. As he turned down the long driveway, he could see two men under the shade of a large oak tree. The men were obviously gravediggers. One stood beside a backhoe; the other leaned on a shovel.

The young pastor approached the two men. Though his dark suit and the Bible in his hand gave him away, he still felt the need to explain that he was a pastor.

"Is the family here?" the minister inquired.

"Nope, just left."

"I see," the pastor said, embarrassed that he was so tardy.

"Please give me a few minutes," he requested.

With that, the pastor moved to the open grave, noticing that the concrete vault was already closed. He read a passage of scripture. Though he dispensed with his prepared sermon, he offered a lengthy prayer. He thanked the men for their patience and drove on to the church for the covered dish dinner.

As the young pastor took his leave, the man next to the backhoe lit a cigarette. He turned to the man leaning on the shovel and said, "I've been in this business for thirty years. This is the first time I have ever seen anybody read the Bible and pray over a septic tank!"

No word on how the covered dish dinner went.

Up a Tree

Climbing a tree is a fascinating adventure.

Our son climbed into the sprawling branches of a magnolia. He failed to notice the hornets' nest attached to the same limb from which he was swinging. He left the tree in a hurry with eleven stings.

One summer, my three brothers and I built a treehouse in the woods behind our home. We used scraps of lumber left over from building the pony barn. The tree house was a triangular platform anchored between three poplar trees twenty feet above the ground.

The structure could accommodate three of us if each of us sat with his back against one of the poplars. Four was a crowd, and the one without the backrest was in peril. Brother Bill demonstrated the danger when he tumbled from the platform, landing flat on his back. He survived the fall unscathed because he landed in a hefty pile of pony manure.

We were reminiscing about the treehouse when our dad reminded us of a craze that made the rounds when he was a boy. At the end of the Roaring Twenties and the beginning of the Great Depression, there was an outbreak of fatigue contests. Tree-sitting competitions were a fad.

Across the country, people attempted to break the record of 156 hours up a tree set by Jack Richards of Kansas City. A chap in Fort Worth fell asleep after several days in a Texas oak. He broke two ribs when he came out of his tree.

Frank Kellner of Waco, Texas, stayed in a cottonwood for more than nine days. After 231 hours, at 4 a.m., Frank went to sleep. When he fell from the tree, he had broken the record. He also broke his arm.

Closer to home, our dad recounted the tale of his oldest brother, Tom, persuading a younger brother, Asbury, to stay on a tree platform for several days. Tom slept in a comfortable bed at night, leaving Asbury high in the branches of a sweet gum.

As the story goes, my grandmother designed a way to bring an end to the tree sitting. My grandfather sat in a rocker on the front porch and passed out Snickers bars to the children who came to get them. Asbury was not to be denied. He came down from the tree to get his candy bar against the vigorous protest of his big brother.

Tree sitting caught on as a fad, especially around the mill villages near our town. The most dramatic episode occurred at the center of town. A big oak tree towered above the Deluxe Diner. The owner of the diner built an eight-foot-square enclosed room in the tree. Electricity and telephone lines were installed. Many of the comforts of home were provided.

The enterprising man took his wife up a ladder and settled her in the tree house. He removed the ladder so she could not come down. The lady seemed content until a thunderstorm rumbled through in the middle of the night knocking out the electricity and the telephone. The woman screamed for help. The fire department came to the rescue. The woman was removed from her lofty abode by a hook and ladder truck, much to the dismay of her husband.

In recent years, tree sitting has become a form of civil disobedience. A protester sits in a tree to protect it from being cut down. Supporters provide the tree sitters with food and necessary supplies.

On May 20, 1985, Mikal Jakubal ascended a Douglas fir in the Willamette National Forest. His protest against clear-cutting the giant trees lasted about a month.

Julia Butterfly Hill, an activist in Humboldt County, California, spent 738 days in a 180-foot, 600-year-old Coast Redwood tree. Hill climbed the tree on December 10, 1997, to protest logging. She thought that she might stay a month, but she didn't come down until two years later, lowering herself from her perch eighteen stories high in the branches of the redwood she called Luna.

In the six-foot-by-eight-foot tree house, Hill spent her days reading, writing poetry, and cooking vegetarian food. She kept fit by climbing the tree's massive, spreading branches.

Treetops Hotel in Aberdare National Park in Kenya, offers guests a close view of African wildlife. Major Eric Walker built the original two-room tree house in a massive 300-year-old fig tree.

In 1952, Princess Elizabeth, and her husband, Prince Philip, visited Kenya. They stayed in the Treetops Hotel as personal guests of Major Walker. While lodging in the treehouse, Princess Elizabeth first learned of the death of her father, King George VI.

The legendary hunter Jim Corbett, a resident of Treetops at the time, wrote in the visitors' logbook: "For the first time in the history of the world, a young girl climbed into a tree one day a Princess. She climbed down from the tree next day a Queen."

Climbing a tree is a fascinating adventure. How we make our descent can determine how we remember the experience. Hornet stings, fractured bones, landing in a pile of pony manure, or being rescued by a firetruck are just not the same as coming down from a tree as the Queen of England.

Please Pass the Tabasco Sauce

One of our treasured family stories is about the first time my mother shared a meal with my father's family. The event occurred two years before my birth. I've heard the tale and repeated it so often I feel almost as if I was there.

The woman who would become my mother was the sweetheart of the man who would become my dad. He took her to a Sunday meal at the family home, the very home in which Clare and I now reside, the home where we reared our own five children.

My dad was one of nine children. The dining room table was large enough to accommodate the entire family. My grandfather, whom I called Pappy, asked the blessing and then grabbed a bottle of Tabasco sauce, shaking the contents all over his salad, a lettuce leaf topped with a pear half, filled with a dollop of mayonnaise, and garnished with grated cheese, and a maraschino cherry.

My mother, seated next to my grandfather, was stunned when she saw her future father-in-law dousing his pear salad with pepper sauce. Noticing her surprise, Pappy quipped, "Louise, if you get ahold of something you don't like, change it to something you do like."

Tabasco Sauce will change the taste of anything.

Edmund McIlhenny, who invented Tabasco sauce, was a banker from Maryland who had moved to Louisiana around 1840.

McIlhenny was an avid gardener. A friend gave him seeds of red peppers from Mexico. At his home on Avery Island in south Louisiana, Edmund sowed the seeds and nurtured the plants to maturity. The peppers they bore were a delight.

McIlhenny created a pepper sauce to add spice and flavor to food. Selecting and crushing the reddest peppers, he mixed them with salt, aging the mash for a month in crockery jars. McIlhenny then blended the mash with white wine vinegar. After aging the mixture another thirty days,

he strained and bottled it.

It proved so popular with family and friends that McIlhenny decided to market his pepper sauce. He grew his first commercial pepper crop in 1868. The next year, he sent out 658 bottles of sauce to wholesale grocers around the Gulf Coast, particularly in New Orleans. He labeled it Tabasco, named for the state in Mexico from which those first seeds came.

McIlhenny secured a patent in 1870, and TABASCO® brand pepper sauce began to set the culinary world on fire.

Labeled in twenty-two languages and dialects, sold in over 160 countries and territories, it is the most famous, most preferred pepper sauce in the world.

Tabasco sauce is still made on Avery Island, Louisiana, at the very site where Edmund McIlhenny planted his first garden. Half of the company's 200 employees live on Avery Island. Their parents and grandparents worked and lived there as well. The current president of the family-owned company is a sixth-generation McIlhenny.

Until recently, all of the peppers were grown on Avery Island. The bulk of the crop is now grown in South America, where weather allows a more predictable supply.

Following tradition, the peppers are handpicked. Peppers are checked with a little red stick, *le petit bâton rouge*, to determine ripeness. Those peppers not matching the color of the stick are not harvested.

Peppers are ground, mixed into mash, and put into old white oak whiskey barrels to age for three years. The bright red mash is so corrosive that forklifts are reported to last only six years.

In addition to the original red Tabasco sauce, several new types of sauces are now produced under the brand name. The company has also cashed in on its name by licensing apparel, including neckties and boxer shorts.

The hot sauce is used to season a variety of foods. It has been used to change the taste of desserts and even pear salad. NASA put Tabasco sauce on the menu for Skylab, the International Space Station, and shuttle missions.

The spicy sauce has appeared in two James Bond movies.

The official Web site of the McIlhenny Company, www.tabasco.com, has nearly 200 pages of stories and comments from Tabasco afficionados. Among the entries are suggestions for alternate uses for the hot sauce:

• Sprinkle Tabasco on flower and vegetable plants to repel pests, especially deer and rabbits.

• Can't get your teenager out of bed to get to school on time? A drop of Tabasco on their lip will awaken them.

• Use a spoonful of Tabasco as a cough remedy.
These comments are included:

• "When I was much younger my grandmother put Tabasco sauce on my fingertips to stop me from chewing my nails. Half a century later, I still bite my nails, and I love Tabasco!"

• "When I was little, if I talked back to momma, she would put Tabasco in my mouth. Soon, I started having a smart mouth on purpose because I loved the taste! To this day I'm just as sassy, and I love Tabasco even more!"

• "My kitchen is full of Tabasco memorabilia. I even named my dog Tabasco!"

• "My husband loves Tabasco sauce so much, he asked me to get a Tabasco tattoo. He thinks it's hot!"

Following the tradition of my grandfather, one of my cousins uses Tabasco on almost everything. I'm not sure if his wife has a Tabasco tattoo or not.

Upstate Strawberries

For an all too brief season every year, locally-grown strawberries take the produce spotlight. Imported berries from California or Florida get us through the colder months, but we look forward to the unsurpassed flavor of Spartanburg County beauties. From Cross Anchor to Cooley Springs, from Chesnee to Lyman, the succulent red strawberries grown on the rolling hills of our county are the fruit of choice from early May through late June.

This is the time of year to visit the U-Pic or We-Pic farms. Some of the best strawberries can be purchased at roadside stands.

I preached a series of sermons at a revival at a country church in the Lowcountry several years ago. On the final night of the revival, we enjoyed a church picnic. At the outdoor picnic supper, an alarmingly large man carrying a dinner-size paper plate sat beside me. His paper plate sagged under a heaping portion of strawberry shortcake. I thought for a moment that the folding chair beneath him would buckle under his weight. When it held securely, I thought the plate of shortcake might be the proverbial straw that broke the camel's back. When the chair withstood the last morsel of the dessert, the man turned to me and said, "Now, preacher, that's the way we're gonna' eat in heaven."

I thought, "Probably sooner than later."

When I was a boy, my Dad was, to my mind, the master strawberry grower. He planted a long, narrow bed of Ozark Beauties next to a stand of tall yellow pine trees. The pine needles provided the mulch to protect the plants in the winter. In the early spring, the pine needles were removed to allow the plant crowns to bud. Delicate white blossoms gave a pleasing portent of the harvest to come. When the strawberries were ripe, we took turns picking. The family rule was to put ten in the bucket for every one you ate. Otherwise the bucket would never have been filled.

From early May until late in June, fresh berries were on our table for three meals a day.

Strawberries brighten the flavor and the appearance a bowl of cold cereal. The red berries sparkle in a salad of fresh fruit. Strawberries over vanilla ice cream are an outstanding ending to a summer supper. Of course, the all-time favorite for many folks is strawberry shortcake. Come to think of it, strawberry shortcake really might be served in heaven.

When Clare and I lived in Louisville, Kentucky, I wanted a small strawberry patch. In the fall, I tilled several bags of composted cow manure into the small garden plot to enrich the clay soil. In the early spring I set out twenty-five strawberry plants and side-dressed them with composted cow manure. My mom and dad came for a visit at exactly the time the strawberries were ripe. Though they were few in number, the berries were plump and delicious. I proudly put a bowl of strawberries in front of my dad, the master at growing strawberries.

He admired the bowl of fresh, red berries, "Tell me what you put on your strawberries."

"Composted cow manure," I said.

He looked at me with a twinkle in his eye and a wry smile on his face. "I think I'll have cream and sugar on mine."

To each his own.

Send Us a Soil Sample

A part of the joy of gardening is digging in the dirt. The good earth can produce an array of beautiful flowers and delicious vegetables, but it needs a little help from the good Lord and the gardener.

The Clemson University Extension Service recommends that gardeners take a soil sample every year. The best time is a couple of months before planting. The test is used to determine the amount of the nutrients essential for plant growth that are present in the earth in your backyard. A test report will also give the pH value of your soil, a measurement of how acidic or basic the dirt is in your garden.

The extension office will ask you to complete the information on a soil test box and fill out a record sheet checking the appropriate items for the analyses desired. The cost of a standard test kit is five dollars per sample. Simply follow the instructions on the box before filling it with dirt and return the sample. The extension folks will make recommendations for the amount and type of fertilizer and lime you need to add to the soil for optimal plant growth. Following their suggestions prevents problems and helps the gardener grow healthier plants.

A retired schoolteacher decided to plant a garden of flowers for cutting and vegetables for cooking. Though she had grown up on a farm in the southern end of our county, she had not worked the earth in years. She read diligently all that she could about gardening. Nearly everything

pointed to the importance of soil sampling. She asked her nephew, a junior high school student, to obtain the sample for her. After an hour or more outside, the boy returned with the sample box filled with dirt.

The woman sent the sealed box, as directed, to the extension service. In about two weeks her report came back. The extension agent wanted to visit her garden. The analysis revealed that the lady's garden was blessed with some of the best soil in South Carolina. The schoolteacher knew something was wrong. Her intended garden consisted of packed red clay. She asked her nephew where he had gotten the sample. "I tried to dig it up out of your yard just like you told me, but the ground was too hard. I found a plastic bag in the garage marked Potting Soil, so I filled the box from the bag. After all, it's all just dirt."

Needless to say, the lady had to repeat the test.

My father-in-law, who grew up during the Great Depression on a red clay farm in Saluda County, South Carolina, could never understand why anybody would pay hard-earned money for dirt packaged in plastic bags. Maybe he had a point.

Several years ago, while visiting the annual Poultry Festival in Leesville, South Carolina, I struck up a conversation with a man from somewhere north of the Mason-Dixon Line. He and his wife had moved to Lake Murray to retire. Though he had worked as a big city executive, he had decided to raise chickens in his retirement. While at the Poultry Festival, he purchased a dozen biddies.

"What kind did you buy?" I asked.

"I'm not sure," he said. "I think the man said they were Red-Eyed Rolands."

I am certainly not an expert on chickens, but I am almost sure he meant to say Rhode Island Reds. I understand the variety is one of the best for laying an abundance of brown eggs.

I heard about a graduate of the University of South Carolina who was so enamored with the Gamecocks that he decided to try his hand at raising chickens. Of course, he wanted a garnet and black variety, but he settled on Rhode Island Reds. After all, fighting gamecocks is illegal in our state. Unlike the retired schoolteacher, the USC graduate knew nothing about farming. He got a friend who owned a tiller to plow a garden plot. He purchased twenty-five biddies from a hatchery and planted the chicks with their heads down in a straight furrow. He watered and fertilized the row of biddies, but much to his dismay, they all died.

He was determined to succeed. "Maybe I did something wrong," he thought. He bought twenty-five more biddies, but this time he planted them feet first. Again he watered and fertilized the row. The chicks did live a bit longer than the first batch, but, again, he had total crop failure. Finally, in desperation and with an enormous effort to swallow his pride, he sent an e-mail to the Agriculture Department at USC's arch-rival, Clemson University. With great humility, he explained how much he wanted to raise chickens that reminded him of his beloved Gamecocks. He described in detail what he had done in his two failed attempts and asked for their advice.

A day later, he received an answer from a graduate assistant in the Agriculture Department at Clemson.

The reply read simply, "Send us a soil sample."

Blue Jay Feathers

Sally Middleton is a North Carolina artist who specializes in wildlife paintings. When I first became familiar with her work, I noticed in almost all of her paintings a single blue jay feather. I knew that there must be a story behind this pattern in her work. Blue jays do not enjoy the best reputation in the world of ornithology. Legend says that on Fridays this raucous bird carries sticks to the Devil to keep the fires of Hell stoked. Why, I wondered, was Sally Middleton so consistent in including a blue jay feather in her paintings?

I later learned the story. One gray day, burdened with family problems and financial concerns, Sally Middleton took a walk in the woods near Asheville, North Carolina. As she walked, a blue jay feather floated down in front of her. She caught it in her hand and took it as a gift of grace. From that day on, the blue jay feather was her personal symbol of hope.

I have told the story many times. I mailed to Sally Middleton a copy of a sermon in which I used her story as an illustration. Her kind response was that the blue jay feather had become a source of hope for many others who treasure her paintings.

Several years ago, I was asked to participate in a funeral service for a young man who died in a drowning accident during the first month of his senior year in high school. His death, of course, was very difficult for his family, especially for his parents. The funeral service was at a Methodist church filled to overflowing with teenagers, parents, and teachers, as well as family friends. The body was cremated for the committal at a camp where this young man had spent several happy summers.

The committal service was for family and a few close friends only. I was invited to travel to the camp to lead the service at a beautiful spot beside the lake. I had been trying to think of a symbol of hope for the parents and siblings of the young man. As I walked along a path through the woods, I found one blue jay feather and then another. Picking up both feathers, I

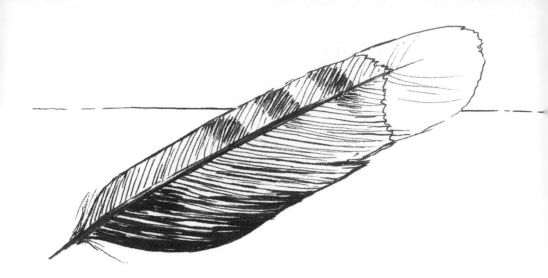

put them in my Bible. When we arrived at the burial site, a shovel with a stirrup handle had been pushed into the ground behind the simple wood and brass urn containing the ashes. The shovel stood like a marker above the place of interment.

At the gravesite, I read scripture and shared the story of Sally Middleton. I gave both the father and the mother one of the blue jay feathers, suggesting that they might become for them signs of hope. We had a closing prayer including the words of committal. Just as I concluded the prayer, a blue jay squawked, flew through the circle of those gathered, and perched on the handle of the shovel just above the urn. The audible gasp in unison of the assembled mourners gave way to a holy silence. No one made a sound, not even the blue jay.

It was a singular moment of quiet reverence.

Later in the week the young man's mother returned to the camp to place flowers on her son's grave. As she stood weeping with a friend, she was astonished when a blue jay landed on her shoulder. The bird flew away after a moment or two.

The Camp Ranger gave a logical explanation for the blue jay's behavior. During the summer, the camp staff had fed peanuts to the blue jay, training him to perch on their shoulders. When the camping season ended, the blue jay, unafraid of humans, continued to beg for peanuts whenever they visited his domain. For those parents, the reasonable explanation did nothing to diminish the blue jay and his feathers as symbols of hope.

Emily Dickinson wrote, "Hope is the thing with feathers—That perches in the soul."

So it is.

The Hog with the Wooden Leg

Tom T. Hall is a writer and a singer of country music for thinkers. Most of his songs are character studies that inform and inspire. His stories in song reveal an understanding of human nature, the value of ordinary people, and the virtue of overcoming adversity. Among his best known musical titles are "I Remember the Year that Clayton Delaney Died," "Old Dogs, Children, and Watermelon Wine," and, my personal favorite, "The One-Legged Chicken."

The following story reminds me of the kind of tale Tom T. Hall might put to music.

A man was driving out in the county one Sunday afternoon between Pauline and Cross Anchor. He passed a farmhouse, a well-kept, pleasant-looking place. The passerby slowed as he noticed a farmer sitting in a rocking chair on the porch of the attractive home. He saw something else that brought him to a complete stop—an enormous hog stretched out in the yard of this house, and the hog seemed to have a wooden leg.

The traveler could hardly believe his eyes. He turned into the driveway, got out of the car, walked over to the porch, and removed his hat. The farmer invited him to come up on the porch and take a seat. The visitor did just that. He looked again at the hog and noticed that indeed the gigantic swine had a wooden leg. After a few pleasantries, he commented to the farmer, "That's a nice hog you have."

"Yes, sir."

"I noticed that your hog has a wooden leg."

"Yes, sir."

"Would you mind telling me how that hog got a wooden leg?"

The farmer said, "Listen, fellow. That boar is the most amazing animal you have ever seen. That hog will track rabbits better than a beagle hound. I have actually taken that animal up near the mountains to hunt for rabbits. My hog can trail a rabbit better than any dog you have ever seen. He has a little trouble when he comes to a wire fence. Instead of trying to go through it, he just knocks it down. Do you know that last fall I was hunting with this hog outside of Landrum near the mountains? We were out in a field close to the woods, and we got closer and closer to the tree line. A huge black bear came out of the woods and was all over the top of me before I knew it. This hog charged the bear, knocked him down, grabbed the bear by the throat, and killed it. That hog there saved my life. That hog is an amazing animal."

"Yes, I can see that. Tell me," the visitor asked impatiently, "how did he get that wooden leg?"

"You know," the farmer said, "last winter all my livestock was in the barn. It was a very cold night, so I had put a kerosene heater in there. Sometime during the night, the cow kicked over the kerosene heater and set a pile of straw on fire. That hog grabbed a tarp in his mouth pulled it over that burning straw, and smothered the flames. That hog kept my barn from burning to the ground. He saved all of my livestock. Fellow, that hog is an amazing animal."

"Yes, sir, I can see that." Growing even more impatient the traveler pressed for an answer. "Please tell me, how did he get that wooden leg?"

"Last summer," the farmer answered, "My ten-year-old grandson was down at the swimming hole, and he got in water over his head. When he started hollering because he had cramps, that hog dove in the water, came up under my grandboy, and carried him safely to the bank. The boy would have drowned if it had not been for that hog. I tell you, that hog is an amazing animal."

"Yes, sir, I can see that!" the exasperated listener exclaimed. "But I want to know, how did that hog get a wooden leg?"

The farmer paused thoughtfully and asked, "Tell me fellow, if you had a hog like that, you wouldn't want to eat him all at once, would you?"

When Turkeys Become Targets

Last week I saw a wild turkey wandering around in a suburban area of our town. Since this is the third full week of turkey season, I assumed that this magnificent lady was dazed and confused. I find it odd that hunting season for the wild turkey corresponds to the mating season for these spectacular birds. I can think of no other wild game that is hunted during its reproductive season. The hen I saw may have already lost her Tom.

Other wild turkey sightings in populated areas have been frequent. A flock of twenty or more scurried across Fernwood Drive near Lawson's Fork Creek. A dozen of the birds showed up at the Emergency Room entrance to Mary Black Hospital. A doctor, an avid hunter, said, "The turkeys came to the ER because a gobbler had suffered a gunshot wound."

A friend reported two hens crossing our church parking lot seeking sanctuary in a cane break bordering the property. A resident of Duncan Park shared a tale of wild turkeys involving three hens and one jake. Suffice it to say that with hunting season in full swing, there are fewer Toms to go around.

Benjamin Franklin had many good ideas. He played a major role in crafting our Declaration of Independence and our Constitution. However, the Philadelphia statesman had one very bad idea that could have altered the course of history. Ben proposed to Congress that the wild turkey be designated as our national bird.

In their wisdom, Congress chose the bald eagle instead. Imagine how our lives might have been different if the turkey rather than the eagle had become our national symbol.

• Our coins would display the image of a wild turkey instead of a bald eagle.

• The professional football team in Ben Franklin's City of Brotherly Love might not be the Philadelphia Eagles, but the Philadelphia Turkeys.

• When the Apollo 11 Lunar Module landed on the surface of the moon, we might have heard, "Tranquility base here. The turkey has landed."

• The Boy Scouts of America would honor young men with the Turkey Scout Award.

We can all be glad that the eagle is our emblem.

In 1976, the wild turkey was designated South Carolina's official State Wild Game Bird. The turkey season, beginning on April Fool's Day, might be controversial if camouflaged hunters, armed with turkey calls and rifles, were preying on our national bird.

I first heard a story from Dr. Alastair Walker about a pair of eagles who built their nest on a high cliff above a river bordered by dense woodlands. The eggs in the eyrie hatched, producing two fine young eaglets. Before they were able to fly, a ferocious storm swept the face of the rock cliff, demolishing the nest, plummeting the young eagles to the ground.

Talk about dazed and confused! The young eaglets aimlessly wandered through the forest, obscured from the view of their parents frantically soaring above.

The eaglets stumbled upon a flock of wild turkeys. A big Tom approached them, inviting them to join the flock. The eagles traveled with the turkeys, roaming through the woods. They ate acorns and hickory nuts, normal fare for turkeys, but not nearly as appetizing as the fish to which the eagles had grown accustomed.

One day as they were walking through the woods, they heard a voice above, "Whooo are you?" On the limb of a tall white pine tree perched a wise old owl. He repeated, "Whooo are you?"

An eaglet replied, "We are turkeys. We live with turkeys. We behave like turkeys. We eat like turkeys."

"No," said the owl, "you are not turkeys. You are eagles. Be true to yourselves. Be eagles!"

"But we don't know how to be eagles," whined the young eagle.

The owl responded, "You will never be eagles as long as you act like turkeys. Look to the eagles. Become what you were created to be."

With that, the wise old owl pointed with his wing toward the sky. Soaring high above were eagles, perhaps even the parents of the lost eaglets.

"Become like them," instructed the owl.

One young eaglet hopped over to a fallen tree. He climbed up the trunk and out onto the highest branch. There he spread his massive wings for the first time. In one great moment of daring, he flapped those wings. His feathers caught the air, and he rose in flight to join the other eagles high above.

The other young eagle watched as his brother soared out of sight, high above the trees, far above the rock cliff. He thought to himself, *I could never do that.* He looked down on the ground and pecked at an acorn. He tried to make a sound, but it was not even a respectable gobble.

He continued to travel with the turkeys. Then came hunting season. Sadly, the young eagle never became who he was created to be.

We are all created in the image of God. The Creator has a plan and a purpose for each of our lives. To settle for anything less is to be like the eagle who acted like a turkey.

My Personal Philosopher

When Clare and I returned to Spartanburg in 1980, we moved into the home that my grandmother and grandfather had built after the Great Depression in 1937. Soon afterwards, I met the man who would become my personal philosopher.

David lived on the King Line behind the old stockyard, located not far from our home. Though crippled up with arthritis, he would walk from his home past our house on his way to the lumberyard. There he purchased his daily Coca-Cola.

David could barely walk. His feet were so gnarled that they hurt constantly. His gait was more like a shuffle.

In those days, in order to get to the lumberyard, he had to pass a mini-mart. I asked him why he didn't just go there to buy the Coke.

He said, "At the mini-mart, it costs thirty-five cents. At the lumberyard, it costs a quarter. No need wasting money."

Though every step was painful, David walked twice as far just to save a dime.

Often David would stop at my house, sit in a rocking chair on my front porch to enjoy his Coca-Cola, and then shuffle on to his home. Many mornings I would take my mug of coffee and join David on the porch. Those were the times when I received my philosophy lesson.

In his starched and pressed khaki pants, David was always as neat as a pin. One February morning, his knees were covered with mud.

I asked, "David, what in the world have you been doin' this early in the mornin'?"

"Yesterday, I put in my English peas." David grew some of the best vegetables in some of the reddest clay in Spartanburg County. He planted according to the astrological signs.

"David, why are your pants so muddy today?"

"Got up early. Dug up all the seeds."

"Why?"

"My daughter was readin' the Old Almanac. She tol' me I put in my peas on the wrong sign. So, I dug 'em all up this mornin' before daylight."

"Did you find 'em all?"

"Found all but four."

He pulled a paper bag from his pocket with the seeds. He had planted three rows of English peas the day before.

"When's the right time to plant English peas?"

"Tomorrow."

"Will one day make a difference?"

"Yes, suh. My daddy always planted by the signs, and he always made a crop. I do the same."

David was quite a gardener.

David and I were standing in my garden late one summer day. My wife brought each of us a cup of ice water. At the time, Clare was pregnant with our daughter, Betsy. As Clare walked toward the garden, obviously an expectant mother, David said to me, "Don't you let her come in this garden!"

"Why, David?"

"You let a woman with child come in the garden, and every watermelon and cantaloupe will bust wide open."

Clare had no intention of coming into the garden. She handed our ice water over the fence.

David always kept a salt shaker with him in the summertime. Occasionally, he removed his old stained hat and sprinkled a little salt in his hair. He said the application of salt kept him from passing out.

I do not know whether that works or not. David never passed out, and I saw him sprinkle a good bit of salt in his hair.

David was quite a churchman, too. He loved going to church. He especially enjoyed singing in the choir. On Monday mornings, he would give me a report from the Sunday services.

One Monday we were having our early morning porch visit.

"Church was extra good yesterday."

"What was good about it?"

"We had good singin'." David always bragged on the choir.

"How was the preachin'?"

"Preachin' was good."

"What'd the pastor preach about?"

"Well, he preached about sin."

"What did he have to say about sin?"

"He's agin' it!"

"What kind of sin did he talk about, David?"

"He talked about gamblin'. He talked about drinkin'. He talked about smokin'."

"Did he say that smokin' is a sin?"

"Yes, suh."

David dipped snuff. He almost always had tobacco tucked in his lower lip.

"Did the preacher say anything about dippin' snuff?"

"No suh. He didn't say a thing about dippin'."

"David, is it a sin to dip snuff?"

"No, suh."

"It's a sin to smoke, but not a sin to dip snuff?"

"That's right."

"Why's that? How can smokin' be a sin, but dippin' snuff not be a sin?"

He said, "It's a sin to burn up anything that tastes that good!"

David's church built a new sanctuary. He invited me to come to the dedication. My dad and I went together to the Sunday afternoon service, all three hours of it.

David sang in the choir. Several preachers held forth. The building was thoroughly dedicated.

After the service, David showed us around the church he took so much pride in. He explained that the church didn't have stained glass windows. I will never forget the way that he expressed it.

"We don't have none of them windows with people on 'em that the light shines through."

When you know people like David, you don't need stained glass windows. David was the kind of person that the light shined through.

Roadkill

These warming late spring and early summer nights bring critters out of the woods and fields and onto the roads where gasoline-powered danger lurks. A recent early-morning drive down Highway 56, through Pauline and Cross Anchor to Clinton, gave a casualty count of two possums, two raccoons, one squirrel, one black snake, one gray fox, and several stray dogs and cats. It's a rough life out there where "highways become die ways," to use a slogan coined by the South Carolina Highway Patrol.

Roadkill provides the meat (pun intended) for a few tongue-in-cheek recipes and any number of Southern jokes. Maybe you have heard this joke: How many people from Spartanburg County does it take to eat a possum? The correct answer is three—one to eat, two to direct traffic. Or maybe you have heard the one that goes, Why did the chicken cross the road? To show the possum it could be done.

Roadkill can be hazardous to the driver, as well as to the critter. A friend in North Carolina collided with a red-tailed hawk that splattered across his windshield. Blinded by the feathers, he swerved into a ditch, inflicting several hundred dollars of damage to his car. The demise of the poor hawk, a protected bird of prey, was a tragic loss. Any driver who has had the misfortune to hit a white-tailed deer knows all too well the perils and the expense of such an encounter. Bumper-mounted deer whistles are a good investment.

Fishermen friends and I were traveling to Lake Murray before dawn one June day. Out of the darkness, a small doe leapt into the side of our car. The unfortunate animal was killed instantly. Her body damaged the passenger side fender and hood; her head shattered the windshield. We waited for a state trooper to make an official report so that my friend's insurance company would pay for some of the damage. Afterwards, the trooper put the deer in the trunk of his patrol car and drove to a venison processing plant near the accident. Some people really do eat roadkill.

Several years ago, on a late-night drive back from the beach, the driver of the eighteen-wheeler in front of me slammed on his brakes and came to an almost complete stop. A mother skunk was ushering her seven or eight babies across I-26. The black and white family clearly had the right of way. Fortunately, the eighteen-wheeler and I had that stretch of road to ourselves. It occurred to me that the big truck would probably not have slowed at all for only a single skunk. The four-lane interstate would have again become the site for yet another smelly roadkill.

I have witnessed other times when traffic stopped for a family of creatures in the road. On Highway 176, between Pacolet and Union, four lanes of traffic paused while a flock of seventeen or so wild turkeys ran and flapped their way across the asphalt. One dark night on Highway 25, near the Greenville watershed, I stopped and gazed in amazement as a wild sow and perhaps a dozen piglets scampered through the beam of my headlights. A single death may seem of little consequence, but something about seeing a family of creatures in harm's way brings us up short.

Two weeks ago while traveling to a church camp in Greenville County, I rounded a curve somewhere beyond Campobello and Gowansville on Highway 11. There I saw an elderly couple refreshing the artificial flowers on a wooden cross, placed as a memorial just off the shoulder of the road. The cross, I am sure, marked the site of the death of a person they loved. I have no way of knowing their story. I do know that their loss, like every death, involves a family.

When you stop and think about it, roadkill is really not very funny at all. For those who have lost loved ones, death on the highway is a heartbreaking reality. Please be careful. We don't want to lose a single one of you.

The Death of a Beagle

When I was nearly seven years old, the oldest of five children, our family moved to a larger house surrounded by open fields on three sides and deep woods in back. Though Mama had her hands full caring for our family, Dad knew that it was time for me to have a dog. My birthday gift was a beagle pup. I named her Katie. She was an outside dog because that was the only kind Mama would allow. Katie's favorite pastime was chasing rabbits. Many a morning I was awakened by her hound dog howl as she ran a rabbit through a field and into the woods.

Just down the road from our place was a dairy farm. The farmer depended on contented cows to give sweet milk. When Katie could not scare up a rabbit for her early morning run, she was always able to find a cow or two to pester. Early one spring morning, I heard her baying, followed by a rifle shot, then by silence. Worried, I quickly dressed and hurried downstairs. Dad already had Katie settled in a cardboard box. She was injured and bleeding. We carried her to Dr. Ed Brown, a family friend and veterinarian. Dr. Brown, whose son Tommy was my age, took my dad aside and told him that my beagle's back legs were paralyzed and that she would have to be euthanized.

He assured us that Katie was not in pain. His advice was that I take my dog home for a few days so I could pet her and have a little time to say goodbye. She never left the cardboard box. Her beagle eyes were sad; her tail could no longer wag.

A day or two later, Dad said, "Kirk, you know Katie is not going to get well."

I knew, and I cried. Once I pulled myself together, I said, "We need to let Dr. Brown put her to sleep." Together my dad and I took Katie in her cardboard box to the vet. The reality and mystery of death confronted me for the first time.

When our children were young, we often had pets, several at a time and

usually a variety. One Saturday morning, we discovered that one of the fish in the aquarium in our den had died. Together the children and I removed the dearly departed Swordtail from the tank, carefully placed him in a matchbox lined with tissue, and ceremoniously took the contrived casket to the flowerbed. We dug a hole, sang "Shall We Gather at the River," had a prayer, and buried the box.

Back inside, we discovered another fish had gone belly up. This time, there was less ceremony. We wrapped the second Swordtail in a tissue, with none of the reverence afforded the first, and deposited him in a shallow grave.

Upon our return to the den, we found yet another dead fish. It seems one of our sons had discovered that pecans would float in the fish tank. No doubt, the pecans shells had been treated with a pesticide, and we were suffering a fish kill in our aquarium.

This third death called for even less ritual. Our seven-year-old reasoned, "Dad, this fish has lived in water all of his life. I think we should bury him at sea." We flushed the third Swordtail down the toilet.

A fellow pastor and good friend shared with me an experience from early in his ministry in a rural church. It seems an eight-year-old boy had a pet beagle, Barney. Each morning Barney followed the boy to the bus stop. Barney met the school bus every afternoon. The boy and his dog played together each day after school.

One winter morning, after the school bus drove away, the beagle followed his nose into the highway and was killed by a dump truck. The boy's mother, concerned about her child's certain grief, asked the young pastor to be at the farmhouse when her son returned from school. Inexperienced but eager to help, the pastor did all of the talking—far too much talking.

The gist of his fifteen-minute explanation was, "Barney was in the road. A dump truck ran over him." The young minister, compromising and confusing his own beliefs, concluded, "Jesus has taken your dog to heaven." The pastor finally paused with, "Son, do you have any questions?"

The boy thought for a moment, sniffled back his tears, and inquired, "Preacher, what does Jesus want with a dead dog?"

Amazing Grace Wind Chimes

On a recent trip to the South Carolina coast, my wife and I stopped for breakfast at a place that has become a familiar landmark along interstate highways. We put our names on a waiting list. Tables for two in the non-smoking section are in high demand. Fortunately, this particular establishment has an array of rocking chairs on the front porch for those who prefer to sit outside and wait. The rocking chairs, by the way, are for sale. Inside the building, those who wish to eat must make their way through a maze of merchandise on display. As Clare and I waited for our name to be called, we chose to browse. I discovered a rack of wind chimes.

Wind chimes are a favorite at our house. Clare's father, who made the first ones I ever saw, fashioned them from conduit pipe and small gauge chain. The entire assembly was fastened to a piece of square wood with screw eyes and S hooks. Though he died in 1984, we still enjoy the sound of those chimes whenever a breeze blows.

The art of making wind chimes has gone high tech. Chimes have been tuned to sound like Gregorian chants or eastern temple bells. Chimes have been tuned to the first few notes of Vivaldi's "Four Seasons." I found wind chimes on the rack at the restaurant tuned to the first few notes of "Amazing Grace."

I showed the "Amazing Grace" wind chimes to Clare. She suggested we buy several sets.

We gave one set to my sister and brother-in-law who live in Mount Pleasant, South Carolina. My brother-in-law, Terry, has given us a report: "If I sit on my screened porch with a cup of coffee and listen carefully while a gentle breeze is blowing, I really can hear a suggestion of 'Amazing Grace.'"

He smiled and continued, "The other night we had a big storm. The 'Amazing Grace' wind chimes rang like crazy, and twenty-five people in our neighborhood came to our door looking for the revival meeting."

Most people know that John Newton wrote "Amazing Grace." His father was a sea captain, and John became a sailor as a teenager. By the time he was twenty years old, he was the captain of his own slave ship. For nine years, he bought and transported Africans in the slave trade.

On March 21, 1748, in the midst of a storm, Newton prayed to God for deliverance. The experience changed his life. John Newton left the sea and eventually entered the ministry. His memory of that night at sea later led him to pen the words of the hymn "Amazing Grace."

Newton's words were put to the melody of an African slave song, a song Newton had heard many times rising from the hold of his slave ship. For generations, "Amazing Grace" has been sung in rural churches and in city cathedrals. Shape-note singers in Southern revivals have harmonized it. Native American flutes have played it. The Harlem Boys Choir has performed it. Cherokee Indians sang it on the Trail of Tears. Johnny Cash included "Amazing Grace" in nearly all of his prison performances. It never failed to move hardened criminals to tears.

In 1970, folksinger Judy Collins released her version of the song. Her clear, beautiful voice carried the song to the top of the pop music charts. Since that time, it has become the world's most popular religious tune. Judy Collins credits the song with helping her overcome her own problems with alcohol.

On June 11, 1988, in Wembley Stadium, London, England, various musical groups, gathered in celebration of the political changes in South Africa. For twelve hours, rock bands like Guns 'n' Roses blasted away. The crowd was loud and rowdy. The promoters of the event had asked Jessye Norman, an opera singer, to perform the final number. A single spotlight followed this stately African-American woman

onto the stage. With no musical accompaniment, alone and a capella, Jessye Norman began singing.

> *Amazing grace! How sweet the sound,*
> *That saved a wretch like me!*
> *I once was lost, but now am found,*
> *Was blind, but now I see.*

Seventy thousand people fell silent. Jessye Norman began the second verse.

> *'Twas grace that taught my heart to fear,*
> *And grace my fears relieved;*

By the end of the verse, the crowd was entranced.

By the time she got to the third verse, several thousand people were singing with her.

> *'Tis grace hath bro't me safe thus far,*
> *And grace will lead me home.*

Remembering words they had heard in the past, the crowd was transformed into a congregation as they sang the final verse.

> *When we've been there ten thousand years,*
> *Bright shining as the sun,*
> *We've no less days to sing God's praise*
> *Than when we first begun.*

Jessye Norman later said that she felt an unseen power descend on Wembley Stadium that night.

Whether "Amazing Grace" is played on Scottish bagpipes or on a blues harmonica; whether it is sung by the untrained voice of a cotton mill worker or by the Mormon Tabernacle Choir; whether it is played on a pipe organ in a great cathedral or on wind chimes in a summer breeze, the hymn is a reminder of God's love.

When grace descends, the world falls silent, and human lives are changed.

On Being Stung

In the year 1918, some ninety years ago, a group of illegal aliens entered this country. They were stowaways on a ship arriving from South America. They entered unnoticed through the port of Mobile, Alabama. These immigrants soon became migrants, spreading throughout the South. They were a prolific lot, producing many offspring. Moving north and east and west, they eventually reached South Carolina.

A while back, I encountered these aliens while I was in my garden. As I was planting an aster, I disturbed a colony of these pesky intruders. Immediately my left arm was covered with a swarm of Solenopsis invicta.

Black fire ants are nasty little critters. They lock their jaws into your flesh and inject venom with the other end, biting and stinging simultaneously.

The United States Army recommends bleach as first aid. I keep a bottle in my tool shed. I poured Clorox on both arms, waited a few minutes, and washed it off with cool water. I took Benadryl to try to help with the itching. All that week, I used a lot of cortisone cream.

As a boy, I got stung ten or twelve times every summer. A sting was an occupational hazard when cutting the grass, hiking, camping, and fishing. My grandfather had a remedy for stings. He would bite the end off his cigar, chew it up, and slather tobacco juice on the wound.

Over time, I have developed an allergy to stinging insects. Now I carry a sting kit that includes Benadryl and a hypodermic of epinephrine, a form of adrenaline. The kit also contains a shaker of meat tenderizer. The powdered tenderizer neutralizes the venom of a stinging insect by breaking down the protein.

Insect stings can be deadly. More people die in the United States every year from insect stings than from poisonous snake bites or from shark attacks. An allergy to stinging insects keeps you on your toes. A general rule is to wear long sleeves and use insect repellent.

Several years ago I traveled with a group of twenty-three men to raft down the Nolichucky River. As I stepped out of the van at the outfitter in Erwin, Tennessee, a yellow jacket stung me on the leg. One of the men had wad of chewing tobacco. He applied the familiar poultice. It didn't help at all.

I was experiencing my first severe allergic reaction. I turned fiery red all over. Knots developed on the back of my head and neck. My breathing became labored. There in the remote Blue Ridge, by a mountain river, I was in trouble!

Fortunately, numbered among the twenty-three men were my family doctor, a cardiologist, an anesthesiologist, and two pharmaceutical representatives. Before I could turn around, they had given me Benadryl. The cardiologist, family physician, and the anesthesiologist all recognized that I was having a severe anaphylactic reaction.

The three physicians drove me in a four-wheel-drive vehicle along a rugged logging road over a mountain to a drugstore in Erwin. We were a motley crew, dressed as we were for rafting. When my physician demanded the appropriate medications, I am sure the pharmacist thought it was a holdup. My family doctor ordered cortisone, epinephrine, and two hypodermic needles. The pharmacist blinked at him until the doctor pulled out his wallet and presented his credentials. The cardiologist monitored my pulse; the anesthesiologist my breathing. Spread out on the drugstore

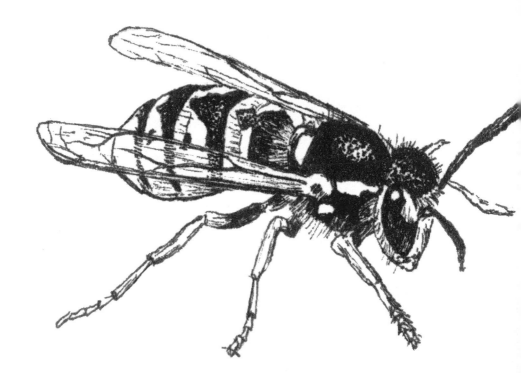

floor, I was given a shot of cortisone in one arm and a shot of adrenaline in the other. Soon, I was just fine.

Chip, the anesthesiologist, told me how relieved he was.

"We had drawn straws to see who might have to give you mouth-to-mouth. I got the short straw."

By the time we made our way back to the river, I was revved up. All three doctors jumped in the raft with me. I don't believe they paddled much at all. I was so pumped up on adrenaline, I paddled nonstop all day long. I had so much cortisone in me that I never felt sore.

Chip, the anesthesiologist, was my fishing buddy. Three years after our experience on the Nolichucky River, we were driving in his old Jeep on a back road in North Carolina, headed to a trout stream that held great promise. As we drove through the countryside, an insect flew into the open window. It looked like a yellow jacket on steroids. It was the largest stinging insect I have ever seen. It was very long, with distinctive black and yellow markings on the abdomen. Though I didn't know what it was, I did know that it was not a good traveling companion. It lit on the dashboard in front of me.

Chip pulled the Jeep over to the side of the road. He reached out his hand and grabbed that insect. It immediately stung him. He threw the critter out the window. He scraped the sting with his pocketknife, put some ointment on it, and then took some Benadryl.

"Why'd you do that?" I asked.

"I barely avoided giving you mouth-to-mouth three years ago. I didn't want to put myself in that situation again. Besides, I want to go trout fishing. If you get stung, it's a big deal. If I get stung, we can still fish."

Let's Sit in the Yard

Early one morning, Clare and I took a few moments to enjoy a cup of coffee on our back porch. We were treated to an outdoor concert.

In the fresh air and sunlight of a spring day, songs of birds filled the air. In a firethorn pyracantha at the corner of the house, a mockingbird sang a medley of at least fifteen different songs, all borrowed from her feathered friends.

A nuthatch made frequent trips to a suet feeder on the other side of the porch, busily feeding her young in her nest, hidden in an oak tree. A black-capped chickadee darted back and forth between the seed feeder and a bluebird house she has rented for the season, a place to rear her brood. A Carolina wren perched on a blooming rose, singing her clear song and tending her nest deep inside a Confederate jasmine vine.

Our backyard is a bird sanctuary. It is home to an amazing variety of songbirds. Cardinals and blue jays are regular visitors. Mourning doves flutter and coo. Tiny ruby-throated hummingbirds make occasional forays to the nectar feeders. A pair of Eastern bluebirds has made a home in one of the cedar nesting boxes.

Zeke was a tobacco farmer in the mountains of Kentucky. His beagle, Luther, was constantly by his side. Zeke had a backyard that featured an old Ford pickup truck propped on concrete blocks. A bare dirt path meandered to his dilapidated barn. Along the way, a small vegetable garden flourished in the sunshine. Two dozen or so free-range chickens and a covey of Guinea hens skittered to and fro. Under a white pine tree that was oozing sap, two oak nail kegs were turned upside down, intended for sitting.

"When things become too burdensome," he explained, "I just sit here in the shade. I call this white pine the tree of life."

It was in that shady spot that Zeke rested after he had worked his garden or stripped tobacco. There he swapped stories with his neighbors. A Mason jar of cool well water and a place in the shade beneath the tree of life became, for Zeke, a restorative.

As he put it, "This is where my tired body and my weary soul catch up with each other."

Every backyard, rustic or refined, needs a place for people to perch. Is anything more comforting than a cup of steaming coffee, savored as you sit in a rocking chair on the back porch? Is anything more refreshing than iced tea, sipped from a frosty tumbler, as you rest in a favorite chair on the patio?

Our yard features a Charleston bench tucked away in a secluded corner of the garden. A double swing provides a place where sweethearts of any age can enjoy the transition from sunset to moonlight.

Gathering on the porch or in the yard is a Southern tradition. We have

several areas for sitting—within a grove of oak trees, beneath an arbor, or on our screened porch. Before the advent of air conditioning and television, sitting outside was relief from the accumulated stress and heat of the day.

Many yards and porches featured clusters of chairs, homemade or store-bought, arranged as an outdoor room. In pleasant weather, the outdoor room was always open and could accommodate extra guests.

Sunday was a day of rest. Sunday afternoon was a time for visiting family and friends. Visitors were welcomed with a greeting, "Sit down and stay awhile!"

Outdoor hospitality, Southern style, should include a few amenities. My resident hostess, Clare, keeps a basket positioned near our outdoor living area. The basket is stocked with insect repellent and a citronella candle. A bottle of homemade bubble mixture is available for visiting children. Several fans, the non-electric kind, some fashioned from palmetto fronds and some obtained from funeral parlors, are within easy reach. Of course, Clare offers our guests something cold to drink.

Hospitality is not the only function of a backyard sitting area. In a gentle rain, a shed with a tin roof becomes a musical instrument. It also provides shelter for an artist to set up an easel or sit down with a sketchpad. A writer finds there an old table and ladder-back chair—a place to work on a laptop, crafting words in peace and quiet. A poet kicks back in a hammock until the muse visits and thoughts become verse scribbled in a journal. The artist, the writer, and the poet are not the only ones who need privacy. All of us need some solitude.

The backyard can become a sanctuary, not only for the birds, but also for the weary in body, mind, and spirit. Most of us need some time alone, to meditate, to pray, or to ponder. Sitting outside may give us a ringside seat to a sunrise or a sunset. We may be treated to a concert of singing birds or to the graceful ballet of hummingbirds and butterflies.

This is not a waste of time. Far from it! It is more valuable than many of the other things we might choose to do.

Our yard is a sanctuary indeed.

Maybe Zeke put it best, "This is where my tired body and my weary soul catch up with each other."

Wherever that spot is for you, you will almost surely find your own tree of life nearby.

Sweet Tea Puts Out a Fire

Remember the commercial invitation to "Take the Nestea plunge"? A poor soul, sweltering from the heat, wilting, perspiring, and burning hot, is handed a glass of iced tea. The relief is so immediate and so refreshing that the person falls backward into a swimming pool. The cold drink quenches the thirst, iced tea staves off dehydration, and the plunge puts out the fire.

In her cookbook, *I'll Have What They're Having: Legendary Local Cuisine*, Linda Stradley asserts that there are two kinds of iced teas in the United States. The only difference between the two is sugar. Outside of the southern states, many folks have never even heard of sweet tea, and it is almost always served unsweetened. Here in the South, iced tea is sweet tea and is served year round. For example, our own local Beacon Drive-In dispenses upwards of 3,000 gallons each week, enough to fill an eighteen-wheel tanker truck every two weeks.

A year or so ago, I was walking into the Beacon when I met a friend coming out. He had a large cup of sweet tea in his hand.

"This is my third cup of tea," he boasted.

"You really know how to hold your tea," I said.

"Got to have it. Especially after a catfish a-plenty. Got to have it to put out the fire!"

Barry and Brian are neighbors. Both are fond of sweet iced tea and often enjoy a tall cup of the refreshing beverage while they discuss neighborly issues like home maintenance or lawn mower repair. On a warm afternoon last spring Barry was in his yard sipping his usual super size cup of sweet tea when he noticed smoke and flames pouring from Brian's pickup truck. Barry rushed to the rescue, iced tea in hand. He discovered the fire blazing in the front seat of the truck. Without a moment's hesitation, Barry doused the flames with his precious sweet tea. Apparently, the sugary elixir really does put out the fire.

South Carolina is the first place where tea was grown in the United

States, and it is the only state to have produced tea commercially. The first tea plants arrived in the state in the late 1700s. French explorer and botanist Andre Michaux imported tea plants along with camellias, gardenias, and azaleas. He planted tea at Middleton Plantation near Charleston.

Tea has been served cold at least since the early nineteenth century, when cold green tea punches, heavily spiked with liquor, became popular. By the middle of the nineteenth century, tea punch began to acquire regional names, such as Charleston's St. Cecilia Punch, and Savannah's potent version, Chatham Artillery Punch.

Now the direct descendants of the original tea plants at Middleton Place Gardens have been restored to their former grandeur at a lush, subtropical tea farm, located on Wadmalaw Island. Mack Fleming, a South Carolinian, and William Hall, a British-trained professional tea master, own the 127-acre Charleston Tea Plantation where American Classic tea was developed. The first crop of this new tea was introduced in 1987, and it has gained wide acceptance. The pleasant drink is the sole cash crop of the Lowcountry business. On April 10, 1995, the 111th Session of the South Carolina General Assembly designated South Carolina-grown tea as the Official Hospitality Beverage of the State.

Back in the days when dinner was served at noon and supper came in the evening, sweet iced tea was the beverage of choice at every meal, sometimes even breakfast. Mama always had a big cooked meal fixed in the middle of the day. Meats on a platter, bowls of steaming vegetables, and rolls hot from the oven were served family style. In the middle of the table was a large jar of sweet tea ready to be poured into tall glasses of ice.

One hot July day, Dad and I came home for dinner after a morning's work at the lumberyard. Mama had fixed fried chicken, mashed potatoes, turnip greens, and fried okra. I was so thirsty and did not even wait for the blessing. I found the familiar jar filled with rich amber liquid and filled my glass. I gulped the iced beverage expecting to experience immediate refreshment. Instead, I had a shocking surprise. I could not contain the bitter, burning taste in my mouth. I spewed the liquid back into my glass. About then Mama appeared in the door with hot bread and a jar of sweet tea. In the rush to quench my thirst, I had chugged cider vinegar intended for the turnip greens.

It took a quart or more of sweet tea to put out the fire.

The Gift of Bullfrogs

The water feature in our garden is a favorite place for us to relax. A small waterfall flows down a hillside, spilling into a pond that is lined with creek rocks. The water is recycled back to the top of the hill by a pump, creating a continuous flow. The soothing sound of falling water is like a healing balm to the spirit.

On a recent visit to our garden, a friend sat near the waterfall watching the goldfish swim in and out among the lily pads. "You need a couple of bullfrogs," he said. "Listening to them at night would be a treat." I could recall the pleasant sound of bullfrogs from fishing and camping adventures as a boy. I agreed that a couple of bullfrogs would be a fine addition to our small pond. A few days later a man from our church shared six big croakers from the abundant population in his own pond. "I wanted to be sure you had at least one male and one female," he said.

The gift of frogs was, indeed, a welcomed addition to the garden. I have enjoyed hearing their deep resonant voices singing after dark. One night as I listened, the symphony of bullfrogs and tree frogs, crickets and a persistent whip-poor-will, conjured up thoughts about frog lore and frog stories.

The Bible recounts the part frogs played in the story of the Exodus. God inflicted ten curses on the land of Egypt. One was a plague of frogs. With the land of the Nile overrun by amphibians, imagine the sounds Pharaoh heard at night.

After our gift of frogs arrived,

I learned that a bullfrog can live up to fifteen years and a female bullfrog can lay as many as 20,000 eggs at one time. In a year or so, I may be sharing frogs with some of you.

In 1865, the budding journalist Samuel Clemens was living in a cabin near Angels Camp, California. Better known by his pen name, Mark Twain, he frequented the bar at a local hotel listening to yarns told by prospectors from the nearby hills. The bar is where he heard the tall tale he wrote into a short story about a frog called Dan'l Webster. Twain's legendary amphibian helped make him famous, and he made the frog famous. "The Celebrated Jumping Frog of Calaveras County" is one of the best-known bullfrog stories.

Perhaps the most famous frog story is from the Grimm brothers of fairytale fame. "The Frog-Prince" has been told and retold. Usually the story tells of a princess who finds a conversant frog. The frog asks that she kiss him so that an evil spell can be broken. Then he will become the handsome prince he was prior to the spell. Though in its original form the princess does not actually kiss the frog, it is most frequently told so that a kiss is the act that transforms the frog into a prince.

There are many variations on this theme. One is for liberated women.

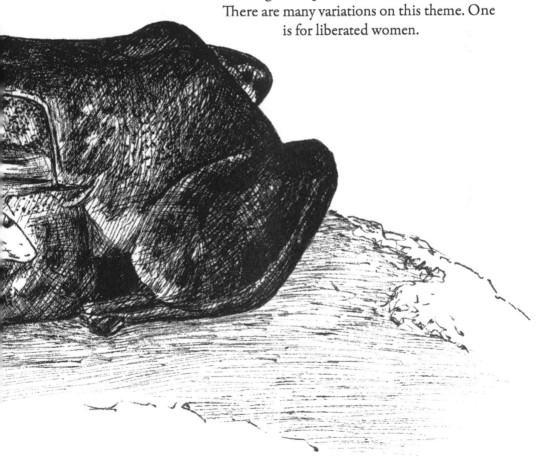

Once upon a time, a beautiful, independent, self-assured princess happened upon a frog in a pond. The frog said to the princess, "I was once a handsome prince until an evil witch put a spell on me. One kiss from you and I will turn back into a prince. Then we can marry, move into the castle with my parents, you can prepare my meals, clean my clothes, bear my children, and we will live happily ever after."

That night, while the princess dined on frog legs, she laughed and said, "I don't think so."

Another variation of the tale is for senior adults.

An old man wearing a tattered long-sleeve shirt, khaki pants, and a straw hat sat on a log. He was fishing with a cane pole from the riverbank. Fishing was slow, and the late summer sun was setting. A bullfrog hopped up on the log next to the elderly gentleman.

"Are you married?" the frog asked.

"No, my wife died five years ago," the man answered, surprised to be speaking with a frog.

After a pause, the frog offered, "I am really a beautiful princess. If you kiss me, I will become a young woman, and I will marry you."

The old gentleman considered the information. Without a word, he gathered his fishing equipment, put the frog into his straw hat, and walked through the dark woods to his pickup truck.

"Are you hard of hearing?" the frog asked.

"No, not at all," the man answered.

The frog repeated, "I am really a beautiful princess. If you kiss me, I will become a gorgeous woman, and I will marry you."

"I understand," the man said.

The frustrated frog spoke loudly. "I am really a beautiful woman. I am offering to become your wife. Why won't you kiss me?"

The old man paused a moment and then explained, "At my age, I'd just as soon listen to a talking frog than listen to a second wife."

Casseroles Are Comfort Food

A while back, I was guest speaker at the Joy Club of Poplar Springs Baptist Church. We had a delightful time together. I especially enjoyed the delicious covered-dish supper. Among the many choices was a variety of casseroles: squash, broccoli, sweet potato, and green bean.

At a recent potluck dinner at the church I pastor, one of our elderly members commented, "I have never seen a church run out of food at a covered-dish supper." His wife offered a ready explanation. "There is always more than enough because people bring casseroles. When you make a casserole, you make a little food go a long way."

In the South, a casserole is the gift of choice brought to the door when a new baby is born or a family is bereaved. One man, still grieving for his mother, told me with a smile that he and his family had enough macaroni and cheese casseroles in the freezer to last a year.

"After my mother died we got fourteen in two days." he said.

When words are inadequate, this ministry of casseroles is a way of expressing love and concern. Think of a casserole as comfort in a dish.

Recently Linda Wertheimer reported on National Public Radio's *All Things Considered* about a nationwide increase in demand for comfort food.

A comfort food looks good, smells good, tastes good, and goes down easy. More importantly, comfort food takes you back to a place where you felt cared for and nourished, a place from childhood associated with a sense of security. In the same way young children become attached to a security blanket, they often latch on to a specific food, repeatedly requesting their comfort food in high stress situations. Adults tend to do the same.

Most comfort foods rely heavily on carbohydrates. Scientists believe that such foods induce a soothing effect in the brain. According to Linda Wertheimer's report, after 9/11 the most common comfort foods chosen in New York City restaurants were chicken potpie, macaroni and cheese, and chocolate desserts.

Jean was the mother of three energetic boys, all teenagers when I knew them. She was a resourceful woman and an excellent cook. On a weeklong youth retreat at the beach, Jean served as our head chef for fifty-two youth and adults. She was the queen of combining bits and pieces of leftovers into gourmet casseroles. "Leftovers," Jean would say, "are like money in the bank. Casseroles are the best way to take a little of this and a little of that to make a tasty meal."

On the last morning of our retreat, we expected a breakfast of cold cereal. Instead, we were served a delectable meal concocted entirely of fragments from the fridge. Jean called her creation a "breakfast divan." Believe me, it was comfort food.

Smart cooks know that, when preparing casseroles, extras can be stored in the freezer for those inevitable unexpected situations. When relatives drop in for the weekend, heating a frozen casserole is a quick and nutritious last-minute dish.

Casseroles are the emergency fund you can eat.

When caring people don't know what to say, they bring food. The more difficult the loss, the more covered dishes come through the kitchen door.

A busy nurse and mother of two often served her family's favorite chicken and broccoli casserole for dinner. Whenever she prepared the dish, she made several, putting extra casseroles in the freezer so they would be readily available in an emergency. Her nursing schedule did not always allow time to cook the evening meal from scratch.

One of her friends gave birth to a new baby, so a gift of food was in order. She placed a chicken and broccoli casserole, still frozen, on a tray in the floor of her minivan. Her plan was to deliver it to her friend's home immediately after she retrieved her son, Joey, from soccer practice. At the soccer field, she discovered that near the end of practice, Joey had been injured. The mother arrived to find him on the ground with the soccer coach attending him.

"He has hurt his right arm," the coach said. "He needs to go to the emergency room."

The nurse/mother looked at her child and his distorted elbow. "We need ice on this to keep down the swelling," she said, taking charge.

"Where can we find ice?" the coach asked.

"Just help me get him to the minivan," the woman directed.

Before driving to the hospital to have the dislocated elbow set, the resourceful mom situated her injured child in the front seat. Folding his sweatshirt across his legs, she put the frozen dish in his lap.

Fastening her child's seatbelt, she said, "Joey, put your elbow down onto the casserole. It will make it feel better."

Casseroles can be comfort food in more ways than one.

Bears in the Upstate

Early Thursday morning, May 29, 2008, a bear was seen roaming along Woodruff Road in Greenville County. The black bear somehow found its way into a dense patch of woods near The Shops at Greenridge, just off of Interstate 85. The bear eluded wildlife officers and has not been seen since. One wildlife official commented that these occasional bears reported in the Upstate are usually juvenile male bears in search of new territory.

"We don't worry too much about them as long as they keep moving."

Nan Lunden, writing for *The Greenville News*, reported that May and June are prime time for black bear sightings in the Upstate.

Skip Still, from the South Carolina Department of Natural Resources, said, "Bears that are born in January aren't pushed out until the next spring. Females don't want them around while they're breeding, and sometimes big bears will kill younger ones. June is usually the breeding season, and females are pushing the adolescent males out. It's analogous to the teenager going off to college."

For some it is the college of hard knocks. Highways pose a threat to young bears leaving their dens. On June 2, 2008, a law enforcement officer shot a male black bear sometime after midnight off of Highway 176 in Spartanburg County.

"The bear had been struck by a vehicle, and veterinary care wouldn't have saved him," Still said. "We don't want animals to suffer."

Another black bear was struck and killed by a vehicle in Anderson County on Interstate 85 about 11:30 that same night.

Bears have been seen recently in Aiken, Gray Court, Columbia, Greenville, and Spartanburg. So far this year, the Department of Natural Resources has had eighty-one reports of bears in populated areas of the Upstate. That is more than double the number at the same time last year.

The state's chief black bear biologist, Skip Still, said bears are increasing both their numbers and their range. He estimates there are 900 bears in the mountains and between 200 and 300 in the Upstate. Last year, licensed hunters killed fifty-eight bears during the two-week hunting season. "The harvest follows the pattern we have been seeing for years and follows all of our indicators," said Still. "We have been telling folks that the black bear population in the mountains and piedmont is expanding both in number and range, and all indications—surveys, human/bear interactions, sightings, road kills—confirm those statements." Every bear harvested last year was in good health. Eight bears were over 400 pounds, with the heaviest weighing 530 pounds.

The largest male bear on record in South Carolina weighed 594 pounds.

About twenty years ago, I was backpacking with a group of Boy Scouts on the Appalachian Trail along the border between North Carolina and Tennessee. At a place named No Business Knob, we stayed awake most of the night listening to a bear tear apart a rotten log. The next morning we concluded that we had no business being on No Business Knob.

One scout said in relief, "At least we don't have bears in Spartanburg."

Twenty years ago bears in the Upstate were rare. I remember one being killed by an eighteen-wheeler on Interstate 26 in the southbound lane between the Landrum exit and the South Carolina Welcome Center.

About ten years ago, residents on Heathwood Circle on the east side of Spartanburg were surprised when a black bear wandered into their neighborhood. The young male had apparently traveled down Lawson's Fork before investigating a garbage can in someone's backyard. The animal was tranquilized and transported back to the mountains.

Black bears travel into the Upstate from the mountains making their way along streams. They may take shelter in culverts and dense thickets. About eighty percent of a black bear's diet is plant matter such as berries and nuts, while the other twenty percent is made up of insects and meat.

While one swipe of a black bear's powerful front paw can kill a full-grown deer, bears much prefer grub worms to venison. Attacks on humans are rare. When a bear attacks a person it is usually because a bear has been provoked, or a mother bear believes her cubs are threatened.

Nobody has been attacked or killed by a bear in South Carolina for many years.

Skip Still offers a unique perspective for all of us to consider. "Bears can learn to live with humans. Can humans learn to live with bears?"

Bear sightings have been reported in every Upstate county during the past ten years. The population of black bears in the northern portions of Oconee, Pickens, Greenville, and Spartanburg counties is increasing. Bears have ranged further south into Anderson, Abbeville, Laurens, Newberry,

Greenwood, McCormick, Saluda, and Edgefield counties.

"I guess they've hit their saturation density, and they're moving out," Still said.

On Friday morning, May 23, 2008, David and Barbara Nivens of the Green Acres neighborhood were disturbed by a commotion outside their bedroom window. A 300-pound black bear had stopped by for a visit. The furry interloper made a hasty departure toward the Springfield Subdivision.

Dawn Neely, my sister-in-law, is the principal at Hendrix Elementary School, less than a mile from where the bear sighting occurred.

"All of the children were safe," Dawn said. "But for the very first time in my career, we had a bear lockdown."

The first, but maybe not the last.

Dead Horse Canyon

The late Dr. Larry McGehee, former vice president of Wofford College, wrote a fine book entitled *Southern Seen: Meditations on Past and Present*. Published by the University of Tennessee Press, it is a collection of his newspaper columns, written over several years and published in small newspapers across the South. I have been reading his book as a companion to my daily devotions.

One of Larry's pieces is entitled "Gullies." There are places across the South where erosion has washed away the soil and dug deep scars into the earth. Larry remembers, as I do, playing cowboys and Indians or capture the flag in these inviting ravines. He recalls a deep gully that undercut a barbed wire fence. The gulch was wide and deep enough to safely drive a tractor under the fence strung high overhead.

In my memory, there are two such landmarks in Spartanburg County. One near Walnut Grove Plantation is completely enshrouded in kudzu. The vine, imported from Japan, doesn't fool anybody. Underneath that mat of green, the shape of the gully can still be discerned. The trees surrounding the edge of the hole are also draped in the kudzu and rise like grotesque topiaries.

The other memorable gully from my childhood we knew as Dead Horse Canyon. It was located behind old Cooperative School House, deep in the woods. Now that area is between a new subdivision and a shopping center. Dead Horse Canyon was a gully that took on mythical proportions in a boy's imagination. It had steep, red-clay sides and was a labyrinth of twists and turns. There lurked an adventure behind every bend. It got its name because somebody in times past threw the carcass of a dead horse down its steep side when what was, no doubt, a reliable animal had to be put down. After buzzards, possums, beetles, and maggots had done their work, the bleached bones of the old horse remained for years.

When I was a boy, my companions from Duncan Park and I made

frequent forays to Dead Horse Canyon. We had to cross a creek by walking on the log of a fallen tree or swinging across on a vine tangled in the treetops. Following the winding path up through the woods, we came to that deep red scar on the hillside.

I once found a king snake in the bottom of Dead Horse Canyon, the biggest one I've ever seen. He had just about finished swallowing a copperhead. Only a little of the yellow tail and the distinctive markings of the viper showed dangling from the king snake's mouth. I gave him a wide berth. I thought anything that could kill a copperhead ought to be left alone.

Dead Horse Canyon was the place where we played out Audie Murphy movies and the stories of the United States Cavalry and Rin Tin Tin.

I remember the shocking discovery that we were not the only ones who knew about Dead Horse Canyon. The boys from Washington Road had their own path to the place. We had one memorable dirt clod fight with them. The skirmish ended in a draw. We agreed to a temporary truce, but also agreed that we would fight again. Our only rule was we couldn't hit anybody in the head, at least not on purpose. Dead Horse Canyon was the venue where laundry detergent commercials would have met their match.

The sad day came when old cars and construction debris started appearing in our canyon. It was as if the grownups in our world had no respect for holy ground. Dead Horse Canyon eventually became a dump.

Dead Horse Canyon is now grown up with trees, partially filled in, and all but gone. Now as an adult standing on what once was the rim of the gully, within view of a four-lane highway, the place doesn't look anything like I remembered. In my boyhood memory, our gully rivaled The Grand Canyon. Even after all these years, I grieve the loss of a landmark from my youth.

The Psalmist declares, "The earth is the Lord's and the fullness thereof" (Psalm 24:1). That surely must include gullies.

Message in a Bottle

In May of 2008, Reid Pannill was walking with his wife in the surf on Fripp Island. The glint of a bottle floating in the tide caught his eye. It was not litter. After prying off the rusted metal cap, the Pannills pulled out notes, handwritten on rolled slips of paper. The clear glass bottle had preserved the messages without damage.

One of the notes read, "I wish for courage to do the things I must do." It was signed by Linda Goodnight. She had written the note on March 11, 1995, and pushed it inside the bottle on the last day of a spring break trip to Edisto Beach.

The Beaufort Gazette reported that the message in the bottle had made the thirteen-year journey along the South Carolina coast, bobbing across St. Helena Sound from Edisto Beach to Fripp Island.

Contacted by the newspaper, Goodnight, now sixty-five, was surprised the message had been found. A middle-aged nursing student when she wrote the note, Linda explained, "Life was changing ... It takes a lot of courage when you're past a certain point in life, to step out there and go back to school and recreate yourself."

Making a wish is only one of the reasons messages are set adrift at sea.

They are also used to study ocean currents. The first documented messages in bottles were released by ancient Greeks.

The experiment showed

that the Mediterranean Sea was formed by the Atlantic Ocean flowing through the Strait of Gibraltar.

In March 2008, Merle Brandell and his black Lab were beachcombing along the Bering Sea. Near his fishing village in Alaska, he spied a plastic bottle on the shore. An envelope was tucked inside with a message from an elementary school student in suburban Seattle.

"This letter is part of our science project to study ocean currents. Please send the date and location of the bottle with your address. I will tell you when and where the bottle was placed in the ocean. Your friend, Emily Hwaung."

Brandell, a bear-hunting guide, found the bottle twenty-one years and 1,735 miles later. Emily, now a thirty-year-old Seattle accountant, was in the fourth grade in 1987 when her message was launched.

Sailors in peril have thrown distress messages into the ocean.

On his journey back to Spain after discovering the New World, Christopher Columbus' ship encountered a severe storm. Columbus sent a report of his discovery along with a note instructing that it be passed on to the Queen of Spain. The desperate message, sealed in a wooden cask, was thrown into the sea. Columbus survived. The cask was never found.

A message in a bottle is often associated with people stranded on a

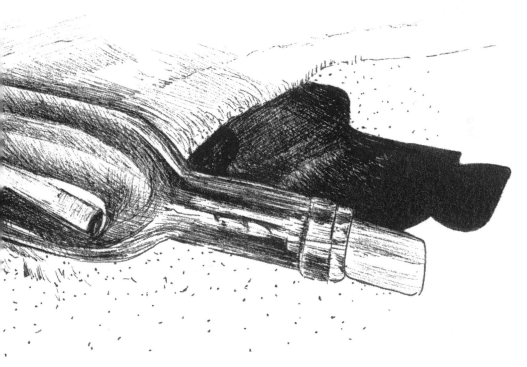

deserted island, hoping to be rescued.

In May 2005, eighty-eight South American refugees, shipwrecked and stranded at sea, were rescued off the shore of Costa Rica. The forty Peruvian and forty-eight Ecuadorean migrants drifted for three days aboard a sinking boat, waiting for help. They had crammed an SOS message into a bottle and tied it to one of the long lines of a passing fishing boat.

A message in a bottle may be the cry of a broken heart.

"Message in a Bottle" is the title of a 1979 song by a rock group called the Police. The song is about a castaway on an island who sends out a message in a bottle to seek help. A year later, he has had no response. Then, he sees a hundred billion bottles on the shore, from people all as lonely and isolated as he.

Micheal Larsen, a rapper known as Eyedea, sings a hip-hop song, "Bottle Dreams." It is the story of an abused violinist, who, in her despair, daily tosses a message in a bottle into a river. After her death, more than 500 of her bottled messages are found.

Nicholas Sparks' novel *Message in a Bottle* evokes this same pathos. Garrett, a seaman, expresses his grief by tossing bottles containing messages overboard. One is found by Theresa, just three weeks after it begins its journey. She discovers the message during a seaside vacation.

The letter opens, "My Dearest Catherine, I miss you my darling, as I always do, but today is particularly hard because the ocean has been singing to me, and the song is that of our life together."

Enthralled by the mysterious romance, Theresa begins a search that takes her to the coastal town where Garrett lives. In 1999, the book was made into a film starring Kevin Costner and Paul Newman.

A message in a bottle is a source of fascination. A glass bottle, floating in ocean waves for years, enduring storms, surviving crashing surf, seems improbable. A note scrawled on paper, preserved in glass, finally found in the sand, is intriguing.

In 1977, Robert Kraske wrote *The Twelve Million Dollar Note: Strange but True Tales of Messages Found in Seagoing Bottles*. Though I have not yet read the book, I intend to do so, probably during our family vacation at the beach this summer.

I will take long walks in the surf, keeping an eye out for bottles.

I also intend to write a note, seal it in a bottle, and pitch it into the waves.

If you find it, let me know.

Shoeless Joe Jackson

Joseph Jefferson Wofford Jackson was born in Pickens County, South Carolina, in 1888. His father was a tenant farmer and a sawmill worker in the foothills of the Blue Ridge Mountains. When Joe was only three years old, the family moved to Brandon Mill, near Pelzer. He was six years old when he began working beside his father in the mill. Joe never went to school and never learned to read or write. At the age of thirteen, young Joe began working in the cotton mill full-time, and started playing baseball in the textile league, earning $2.50 a game.

He continued playing textile baseball until 1908, when he signed a contract with the Carolina Spinners of the South Atlantic League. It was in a game with the Spinners that he acquired his nickname. He had worn a new pair of shoes that produced painful blisters on both feet. He played the next game wearing no shoes. When the barefooted youngster scored, a fan cheering for the opposing team shouted, "You shoeless sonofagun!" Although he played only one game without his shoes, the nickname, Shoeless Joe Jackson, lasted throughout his career.

Connie Mack, owner of the Philadelphia Athletics, purchased Jackson's contract. Joe played less than two seasons before being traded to Cleveland. In 1911, his first full season, he batted .408. The next two seasons, he was second only to Ty Cobb for the batting title.

In 1915, Jackson was traded to the Chicago White Sox. He led the team to a World Series title in 1917.

After the White Sox unexpectedly lost the 1919 World Series to the Cincinnati Reds, eight players, including Jackson, were accused of losing games intentionally as part of a gambling scheme to throw the World Series. In September 1920, a grand jury was convened to investigate.

Almost every authority who has examined the records indicates that Shoeless Joe was innocent, though several of his teammates may well have been guilty.

Jackson's testified, "I played my heart out against Cincinnati. I made thirteen hits. I led both teams in hitting with .375. I hit the only home run of the Series. I came all the way home from first on a single and scored the winning run in that 5-4 game. I handled thirty balls in the outfield and never made an error or allowed a man to take an extra base. I threw out five base-runners during the series."

The extent of Jackson's participation remains controversial. Jackson maintained that he was innocent.

In his book *Eight Men Out*, Eliot Asinof writes that because Jackson was illiterate, he had little awareness of the seriousness of the conspiracy. He went along only because his family was being threatened. Most damaging, Jackson took $5,000 from the gamblers. After the series was over, he tried to give the money back.

In 1921, in a jury trial, he and the other seven so-called "black sox" were acquitted of all charges related to the scandal.

Resulting damage to the sport's reputation led the owners to appoint Federal Judge Kennesaw Mountain Landis as the first Commissioner of Baseball. The day after the players were acquitted, Landis issued his own verdict. Joe Jackson and his seven teammates were barred from professional baseball for life.

In 1922, Jackson returned to Savannah where he had played minor league baseball and operated a successful dry cleaning business. Joe continued to play for semipro and industrial league teams throughout the South until the early 1930s.

In 1933, the Jacksons moved back to Greenville, South Carolina. Joe and his wife opened a liquor store. One story about Shoeless Joe took place at his business. Ty Cobb and sportswriter Grantland Rice entered the store to buy a bottle.

After Cobb completed his purchase, he asked Jackson, "Don't you know me, Joe?"

Jackson replied, "Sure, I know you, Ty. I wasn't sure you wanted to know me."

A proverb says, "A good name is rather to be chosen than great riches." Deserved or not, Joe lost his good name.

Jackson is still regarded as one of the best natural hitters of all time. His approach to batting had a great influence on younger players, especially on Babe Ruth. His lifetime batting average of .356 is the third highest in baseball history. He excelled in the outfield. He had a powerful throwing arm. His glove was referred to as "the place where triples go to die."

Shoeless Joe Jackson is among the finest athletes the Palmetto State has ever produced. Sadly, he is best known for being a member of a team that cheated, though it is almost certain that he was innocent. Many believe that Joe belongs in baseball's Hall of Fame.

Near the end of his life, Joe said, "I can say that my conscience is clear, and that I'll stand on my record in that World Series. I'm not what you call a good Christian, but I believe in the Good Book, particularly where it says 'what you sow, so shall you reap.' I have asked the Lord for guidance before, and I am sure He gave it to me. I'm willing to let the Lord be my judge."

Shoeless Joe Jackson died in 1951. His last words are reported to have been, "I'm about to face the greatest umpire of all, and He knows I am innocent."

The Mystery of the Brown Mountain Lights

The southern Appalachian Mountains are rich in natural beauty and haunting folklore. Brown Mountain lies in the foothills of the Blue Ridge northwest of Morganton, North Carolina, in Burke County. The 2,600-foot mountain and its mysterious lights have intrigued locals and interlopers alike for hundreds of years.

The fascinating lights have been described as glowing circles of fire, as bright lights resembling exploding fireworks, or as lights shining brightly, then fading to a pale glimmer. Sometimes the lights move, drifting slowly across the mountain ridge. At other times they whirl like pinwheels and then dart rapidly away.

Ghostly legends abound. As far back as the year 1200, each period of regional history has produced a new tale.

According to Native American lore, a fierce battle was fought on Brown Mountain between the Cherokee and Catawba tribes. The Cherokees believed that the lights were the spirits of Indian maidens searching for their warriors slain on the mountainside.

In 1771, a German engineer, the first European to explore the region, reported in his journal seeing the lights on Brown Mountain.

One legend tells of a Revolutionary War soldier, an Over-the-Mountain Man. Returning to Brown Mountain, he found his home destroyed by fire, his family missing. Some believe the spirit of the grieving patriot, still carrying his torch, roams the mountain.

In his book *Haunted North Carolina* Troy Taylor relates the story of a murder in 1850. One dark night, a mountain woman disappeared. Folks thought that the woman's husband had taken her life. The community turned out to search for her body. As the search continued, strange lights appeared over Brown Mountain. Some believed they were the spirit of the dead woman, coming back to haunt her killer.

The woman's husband disappeared. Years later, a pile of bones was found under a cliff on Brown Mountain. They were the skeletal remains of the missing woman. They say the lights have appeared frequently ever since.

Most widely circulated is the legend of a plantation owner from the Lowcountry. Traveling to Brown Mountain on a hunting excursion, the man became lost. One of his slaves came to look for him, faithfully searching with a lantern, night after night. According to myth, the spirit of the old slave still searches the mountainside, his lantern glowing in the night.

A bluegrass song popularized by the Kingston Trio has perpetuated the legend. The words to the chorus are:

> *High on the mountain, and down in the valley below,*
> *They shine like the crown of an angel, and fade as the mists come*
> *   and go.*
> *Way over yonder, night after night until dawn,*
> *A faithful old slave, come back from the grave,*
> *(Searching) For his master who's long gone on.*

No suitable scientific explanation exists. Many have tried to solve the mystery. Theories include the will-o'-the-wisp, methane gas rising from bogs; fox fire, a dim light sometimes seen on decaying wood; St. Elmo's fire, a glowing discharge of electricity usually observed on a ship's mast; luminescent phosphorus; or radium rays. All have been dismissed.

Some have suggested the lights could be fires from moonshine stills on the mountain. Others contend the lights are automobile headlight reflections from Rattlesnake Knob.

The lights have been cited as a manifestation of flying saucers. In the 1950s, Ralph Lael, a Burke County resident, claimed that aliens from outer space living inside the mountain create the lights. The aliens apparently took a liking to Ralph because they invited him inside the mountain and showed him their base. Then, he accompanied them on a trip to Venus.

Scientists have advanced the theory that the lights are a mirage: refracted light from nearby towns in the area.

A United States Geological Survey decided in 1913 that the lights were locomotive headlights from the Catawba Valley. However, three years later, a great flood swept through, washing out railroad bridges, roads, and power lines. The lights on the mountain continued to appear as usual.

Dr. Greg Little videotaped the Brown Mountain lights in 2003. He believes they are earthlights. Photographs from satellites show luminous balls emerging from fault lines. The Grandfather Mountain Fault runs directly under Brown Mountain, lending credence to the theory.

Dr. Don Caton, a professor at Appalachian State University, has vowed to debunk the legend of the lights. He speculates they are caused by reflections of stars above Brown Mountain.

A 1922 study by scientists from Georgia Tech came to this conclusion: the lights defy simple explanations. One thing is certain, the Brown Mountain lights do exist and are a natural phenomenon that scientists have yet to explain.

The best place to observe them is at Wiseman's View, an overlook off Highway 105 above the Linville Gorge. Clear weather with limited moonlight is optimal. The lights have been seen at all hours between sundown and sunrise.

Several years ago, I stood at Wiseman's View in Pisgah National Forest hoping to view the Brown Mountain lights. As dusk gave way to darkness, stars filled the sky.

To the southwest, I saw dozens of flickering lights. I gazed in amazement at the tiny lights moving back and forth, flickering off and on.

I rubbed my eyes, blinking a couple of times, before I realized the lights before me were lightning bugs just like the ones I used to catch as a kid.

Oh, for an empty mayonnaise jar!

Fishing Lessons

On the wall at Dolline's Restaurant in Clifton is a picture of a fifty-pound catfish. The big fish was snagged at a bend in the Pacolet River between the textile mill communities of Clifton No. 1 and Clifton No. 2. The young fellow who caught the fish was using a Zebco rod and reel and a crappie spinner. Those who were with him marveled that he was able to land such a big fish on such a small rig.

Thoughts of a good fishing hole brought back memories of my own youth. I started fishing before monofilament line was invented. The rig I first used was a black braided line tied to a cane pole outfitted with a s ingle hook, a split shot, and a real cork. I caught a lot of bream, my share of bass, and a few catfish using a cane pole. Once I caught a snapping turtle.

The lore of fishing abounds with improbable tales. Every fisherman has a story. To be sure, some of them are exaggerated. Embellishment is a part of the craft of weaving a memorable fish tale.

Our daughter-in-law tells about her first fishing trip. She was only five years old. Her daddy and one of his buddies had planned to spend the afternoon on Lake Murray. Her dad decided to take his young daughter along.

The two men had everything they needed for a pleasant trip. The boat was equipped with a fish-finder. A cooler was well supplied. Rods and reels were in good working order. Fresh bait was plentiful. They had neglected one small detail. Neither man had a fishing license.

The beautiful spring afternoon made a perfect day for catching striped bass. The fish were biting. Before long there were five nice stripers in the live well.

One of the men noticed another boat, still some distance away, moving in their direction. There was little doubt. It was the game warden!

Sure enough, the officer pulled alongside. He could hardly believe his eyes! Two grown men were sitting in the stern enjoying a cold beverage.

In the bow sat a five-year-old girl wearing an oversized orange life vest. She was clutching a rod and reel in each hand. A third rig was plopped across her lap!

Though I have enjoyed deep sea trolling, angling on mountain streams, and fishing the deep waters of large lakes, there is nothing more delightful than fishing in a farm pond. The sounds of crickets and frogs, mockingbirds and crows provide the background music for time well spent. The biggest largemouth bass I ever caught was in a North Carolina pond.

I'll never forget the time that I fished into the night, using a fly rod and a wooden orange popper. Bream were spawning on the bed under a full moon. It took nearly two hours just to clean the bream in our bucket.

My grandfather, Pappy, taught me to fish. At daylight in summer, nearly every day except Sunday, we went to a fishing hole near Walnut Grove. We didn't say much. We fished. I mostly watched him.

To this day when I fish, I spit on my bait.

"For the fish, it changes the smell and flavor of the bait," Pappy said.

That is true, especially if the fisherman smokes cigars as he did.

Pappy taught me not to keep a fish unless it was to become supper. "If you're not gonna eat it, throw it back. That way there'll always be plenty of fish."

He taught me to leave the woods and the water cleaner than when I got there. We picked up trash that others had left.

There was one lesson more important than any other.

When I was ten years old, my grandfather presented me with my first rod and reel. It was a steel rod. The reel was loaded with black braided line. Pappy gave me a few quick lessons on how to cast using a wooden Chub Creek minnow with treble hooks. With great care, my grandfather demonstrated the technique. I was sure I could do it.

With rod and reel in hand, I reached back to cast with all my might. On my very first cast with my new rod and reel, I made the biggest catch of my life. I hooked my grandfather right in the eyebrow.

As a young man, Pappy spent four years in the Navy. There he learned a new language. When I set the hook, he used some of his Navy language. He grabbed the line to create some slack and cut it with his pocketknife, leaving the Chub Creek minnow dangling from his eyebrow and a stream of blood running down his face. He reached in his tackle box for a pair of needle-nose pliers. He carefully rolled the hook completely through his eyebrow. With the pliers, he clipped off the barb and removed the hook from his eyebrow.

Pappy bit the end off of his cigar. He chewed it up, making a poultice for his wound. Once the bleeding had stopped, he tied a new lure onto the end of my line and said, "Now let me teach you how to cast."

That day, I learned an important lesson from Pappy. It was more than a fishing lesson. It was a lesson for life, a lesson in grace.

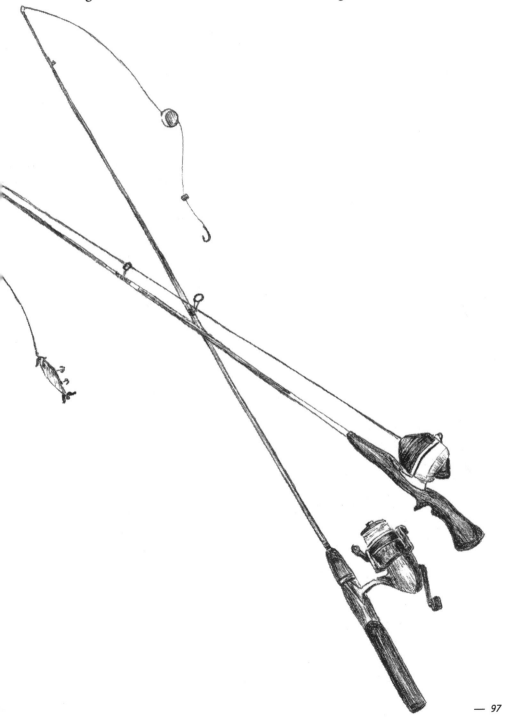

Nothing but White Meat

A distinguishing feature of Southern cooking is the use of pork renderings to add flavor to a variety of down-home dishes, from turnip greens to green beans. We expect to see a piece of bacon curled up in our collards, bits of ham among our black-eyed peas, and small pieces of side meat in our boiled cabbage. We know instinctively that a pot of pinto beans should include a ham hock. Bean with bacon soup is a comfort food in winter, as is a bacon, lettuce, and tomato sandwich in summer.

Our taste for pork violates the teaching of the Old Testament. Jewish dietary law notwithstanding, many of us enjoy "the other white meat," as the Pork Producers Association calls it. On a recent visit to our local grocery store, displayed among pork chops and ribs, I saw split pigs' feet. The sight reminded me of my grandfather's favorite Sunday supper: sharp cheddar cheese, saltine crackers, sardines, and pickled pigs' feet.

In the days when folks still cooked with lard, before any of us had ever heard of cholesterol, we did not know that pork renderings were bad for us. Before bagels and muffins took over, sausage, country ham, and bacon were as much a part of breakfast as eggs, grits, and biscuits. Mercifully, my grandfather died before he knew that many of the things he enjoyed eating were bad for him. He also died before heart catheterizations and coronary bypass surgery were commonplace. Pappy died of heart disease.

Syndicated columnist Lewis Grizzard tells the story of his open-heart surgery in his book, *They Tore My Heart out and Stomped That Sucker Flat*. A valve from a pig's heart replaced one of the valves in his heart. Grizzard, speaking in Spartanburg at a Chamber of Commerce dinner, said, "People ask me if it bothers me that I have part of a pig in my heart. It really doesn't bother me that much, but every time I drive past a barbecue place, my eyes water."

Recently, at a barbeque supper, a friend was reporting on his latest visit to his physician. He, like so many others in our county, has an ongoing struggle with cholesterol and triglycerides. His medical doctor had commented that the Upstate of South Carolina has a rate of coronary disease that is elevated compared to other parts of the country. My friend raised the obvious question, "Why?"

Perhaps because we were having our conversation over a plate of barbeque, I remembered a story told by my grandfather.

A resident of the Pauline community who was both a carpenter and a farmer had a heart attack that just about killed him. The heart attack left the man unable to work. He had always been a good customer at the lumberyard, so my grandfather and grandmother arranged a visit to the home. My grandmother baked one of her fine apple pies for the family.

When Mammy and Pappy arrived, the ailing man was sitting in a ladder-back rocking chair on the front porch. The women went inside the house; the men sat together on the porch.

"How you doing, Captain?" Pappy asked.

"Mr. Ed, I ain't doin' no good at all. This heart attack has left me short of breath. I can't work very much at all."

'What'd your doctor say to do about it?'

"He told me I couldn't eat nothing but white meat."

"No ham or roast beef?"

"No sir, nothing red at all. Just white meat."

"How is that going?"

"Not good at all, Mr. Neely! I'll tell you the truth, I've done eat so much fatback, it's about to kill me!"

No doubt! Old habits die hard.

Scarce as Hen's Teeth

The picturesque town of Leesville, nestled in Lexington County, South Carolina, is renowned for several things. Shealy's Bar-B-Q attracts travelers from near and far with some of the best barbecue pork served in the state. A meal at Shealy's buffet will satisfy even the heartiest appetite. Except for a week in the summer and a week after Christmas, Shealy's is open year-round.

Another of Leesville's claims to fame is the Annual Poultry Festival. Scheduled for late May, the Poultry Festival celebrates chickens. The weekend features carnival rides, concession stands, various contests, music of all kinds, and fireworks. Public places and private residences are decorated with fanciful renderings of the chicken. Some are made from painted plywood. Others are glazed ceramic. Visitors to the Poultry Festival may see sheet metal roosters or papier-mâché biddies trailing behind a mother hen also fashioned from newspaper and glue.

The symbol for the Poultry Festival is a rooster wearing a top hat. Hialeah, Florida, may have pink flamingos as its symbol, but Leesville, South Carolina, has red, white, black, and brown chickens.

The weekend of the Poultry Festival, Shealy's does a booming business. As tasty as Shealy's vegetables are, as savory as their barbecue is, fried chicken is their finest fare. I have eaten Kentucky Fried Chicken at Colonel Sanders' original restaurant in Corbin, Kentucky. Shealy's fried chicken is equally delicious. The cooks in the Leesville restaurant cut whole hens into pieces the old-fashioned way. The pully bones, wishbones to some, are left intact. In fact, it is possible to order a bowlful of pully bones, as well as fried chicken livers, and fried chicken gizzards.

Chickens, like all other birds this side of Jurassic Park, have no teeth. This simple fact, of course, gave rise to the expression, "scarce as hen's teeth." Instead of teeth, birds have a gizzard deep inside, a strong muscular organ that aids in digestion. When a bird eats, food is received in a crop, also called a craw. With the food, the bird ingests small bits of stone and sand. This fact gave rise to the expression, "grit in your craw."

Grit is stored in the gizzard. In the bird's digestive tract, food moves from the crop to the gizzard. The muscular gizzard containing grit pulverizes everything a bird eats, functioning in the same manner as human teeth. Turkey gizzards are strong enough to grind whole acorns and uncracked walnuts. When a chicken is cleaned for cooking, the gizzard is usually split open to remove the grit before the gizzard is cooked. Fried chicken gizzards are considered by many to be a Southern delicacy.

When Lewis Mitchell proposed to Dena Rheney, he presented to her a lovely engagement ring. The modest diamond was beautifully but precariously set in an old-fashioned Tiffany style. Lewis and Dena Mitchell lived in Leesville following their marriage in 1907. The diamond was lost out of the ring several times over the course of their fifty-five year marriage. Once the gem disappeared down the kitchen sink but was later recovered from the curved plumbing trap beneath the counter.

Lewis and Dena Mitchell were maternal grandparents to my wife, Clare. The Mitchell family raised chickens—laying hens for eggs and plump fryers for Sunday dinner.

Dena Mitchell, known to her grandchildren as Mother Dee, prepared her own chicken for frying. Frugal as she was, every part of the chicken was used.

One summer afternoon, Mother Dee noticed that the diamond in her engagement ring was missing. The family undertook an all-out search for the small stone as they had on other occasions. After several days, hope waned. The diamond was lost and was nowhere to be found.

About three weeks later, Mother Dee prepared Sunday dinner for her family. A suitable fryer was selected from the chicken pen, plucked, and cleaned as usual. As Mother Dee cut up the chicken, she came to the gizzard, splitting it open as she always did. She noticed a piece of grit larger than the others. Upon closer inspection, she discovered that it was the diamond from her ring! Apparently, it had dislodged from the setting while she was scattering feed for the chickens weeks before.

A diamond in a chicken gizzard? Such grit in the craw is as scarce as hen's teeth!

The Art of Bricklaying

At a cookout earlier this summer, I admired an outdoor grill made entirely of brick. The owner explained that he had built the grill out of bricks that were left over from the construction of a retaining wall along his driveway. He hired professional bricklayers to build the wall. He watched the masons mix mortar and wield trowels as they crafted the long curved wall. Feeling somewhat confident that he had learned the art of bricklaying by merely watching the skilled laborers, he decided to attempt the brick grill on his own.

"I finally asked one of the men who built the wall to help me with the grill," he explained. "It was not as easy as it looked."

Spartanburg County features several unusual examples of early American brickwork. The Thomas Price house near Switzer was built in 1795 along an old stagecoach road. The steep gambrel roof and two inside end chimneys are distinctive. The brick used in the home were made on the premises and laid in a Flemish Bond style. The restored home is one of our historic treasures.

In the mid-1770s, an itinerant Dutch brick mason traveled through our county. His specialty was building chimneys with a Dutch tapestry design using handmade bricks of differing shades. The light- and dark-colored bricks created a complex pattern of diamonds in a chain. The design runs the entire height of the chimney. Smith's Tavern, also a restored home originally built in 1795, showcases one of the few remaining examples of the Dutchman's craft. The private home is located near the intersection of Ott Shoals Road and Blackstock Road, south of Stone Station.

Foster's Tavern, located along the Old Georgia Road, was constructed in 1807 of hand-thrown brick made from a nearby clay pit. This imposing public house was an elegant inn known for its fine hospitality during the antebellum period. John C. Calhoun was a regular guest at Foster's Tavern, as were a number of other notable travelers. More recently known as the

Ruff House, the landmark stands at the corner of South Carolina Highway 56 and Highway 295 near Cedar Springs.

By the way, the aforementioned clay pit was the place where my grandfather built his home in 1937. It is the home in which our family still lives.

Masonry work requires not only a skilled hand and a sharp eye, but also a keen mind.

Years ago, a math professor from Wofford College came to the lumberyard to buy brick. "I need 5,897 brick," he announced.

My grandfather said, "We usually sell brick by the thousand, but I'll sell you that exact amount for the same price as 6,000."

The professor blinked for a moment before my grandfather added, "That's a lot of brick. What are you building?"

The professor explained that he was building a chimney. My grandfather commented that it must be a mighty big chimney. Then he asked, "Tell me how you figured your brick."

The professor explained that he had measured several brick, and he had measured mortar joints. Multiplying the dimensions of the fireplace and chimney, he had calculated exactly how many brick he needed. "I need exactly 5,897 brick."

My grandfather took a puff on his cigar and said, "I don't know how folks build chimneys where you come from, Professor, but in this part of the world, we usually leave a hole up through the middle of the chimney so the smoke can get out."

An emergency room nurse told me about a patient who came to the hospital in the middle of the night with an apparent kidney stone. After some preliminary tests, she handed the man a small plastic cup and said, "I need a specimen." She left the room for a few minutes.

Upon her return the man was sitting with the empty cup in his hand. He did not understand her request.

She tried to clarify. "Can you make water?" she asked.

"No, ma'am," he said. "I lay brick."

Laying brick is just not as easy as it sounds!

Spiders and Snakes

A boyhood friend spent a week of restless nights on the top bunk at Boy Scout Camp. He fretted the entire time because there were spiders in the cabins and snakes along the trails. Well into his high school years, he wondered about the wisdom of Noah's decision to include tarantulas and cobras on the Ark. Neither his biology teacher nor his preacher could offer satisfactory answers to his questions.

Why did Noah include such frightening animals in his rescue from the flood? Why were they created in the first place? In the lyrics of a popular song, Jim Stafford sings about Mary Lou, a girl he is courting. She expresses the feelings of many, "I don't like spiders and snakes."

Albert Schweitzer was a pastor, physician, musician, theologian, and missionary. In his book *Reverence for Life*, he advocated a philosophy that prevented him from even so much as swatting a mosquito. He lived most of his life in equatorial Africa. No doubt, mosquitoes, as well as spiders and snakes, were a part of his daily experience.

My own philosophy about creepy crawly critters is to live and let live. Whatever the reason, in the created order, spiders and snakes have their place. My problems arise when spiders and snakes become confused and decide that their place is in my place.

In the late spring, I spent most of one Saturday working in my garden. Through the morning, I developed noticeable pain on the top of my right foot. I did not stop to investigate until late afternoon. It is a personality trait I call persistence. My wife calls it stubbornness.

When I finally removed my shoe, I discovered what appeared to be a large blister on the top of my foot. Over the next several days it grew larger, redder, and angrier. When I finally got a medical opinion, I was informed that I had a bite, probably from a black widow spider.

The black widow is so named because immediately after mating, she devours the male. She is a graceful looking spider with a bright red hourglass

marking on her abdomen.

I keep a pair of old shoes on our back porch so I can easily slip into them on my way to the garden. Apparently, a black widow had taken up residence in my right gardening shoe. She regarded my size-eleven foot as an intruder. She expressed her displeasure when I reclaimed the shoe, biting the top of my foot. Clearly, one of us was in the wrong place.

Les Smith is an outdoorsman who lives in the Campobello area. He is a craftsman who fashions beautiful walking sticks from sweet gum saplings. He tramps through the woods to gather armloads of sticks. Examples of his handiwork can be found at gift shops across the Upstate and in Western North Carolina. His walking sticks usually feature the carved face of a bewhiskered mountain man.

Les and his wife, Marnie, are my good friends. When they learned of my spider bite, Marnie recited the litany of bites Les has endured. Last summer, he was hospitalized and received extended treatment for the bite of a brown recluse spider. That was followed by a case of Rocky Mountain spotted fever that Les contracted from a tick. This spring, returning to his truck after going deep into the forest to cut sticks, Les was weaving his way through thick underbrush. He passed a rotten stump, kicking it with his boot, and disturbing a timber rattler that nailed him on the thigh. Again, he was hospitalized. He was treated for the snakebite.

In all, Les has been the recipient of bites from two black widow spiders, one brown recluse spider, three rattlesnakes, and one copperhead. The case of Rocky Mountain spotted fever is insult added to injury. Concerning spiders and snakes, Les would be the first to say that when he goes into the woods, he ventures into their place.

Last week, I saw a spider scurrying across our kitchen counter. After I swatted it into oblivion, I spied the distinctive bright red hourglass on her belly. Our kitchen counter is the wrong place for a black widow spider.

Several years ago, Clare and I undertook the task of cleaning out our basement. We worked together for several hours discarding things we should have thrown out long before. Back in a dark damp corner I saw what looked like an old bungee cord. Just as I reached for it, the bungee slithered away. Yikes!

I searched for several hours to no avail. We salted the basement with mothballs in an attempt to expel the snake. We were careful every time we entered the basement, of course.

Nearly a year later, Clare called me at the office. She had gone to the basement to dry a load of laundry. Coiled in front of the electric clothes dryer was an emaciated snake. I rushed home to find Clare confronting a small copperhead. I promptly beheaded the viper. Copperheads have their place, but it is not our basement.

I was at a question and answer session with Rudy Mancke, host of the successful television series *Nature Scene*. Rudy was asked the question my friend from years before might have posed. "Why did God create copperheads?"

Rudy grinned. "To keep sissies out of the woods!"

The Dog Days of Summer

How hot is it? Among other answers I have heard during this week of record high temperatures are:

"Hotter than a two-dollar pistol!"

"Hotter than a forty-dollar mule!"

"So hot that when I dug up potatoes in my garden, they were already baked."

"So hot that we had to feed the hens crushed ice to keep them from laying hard-boiled eggs."

Last week, during the nationwide heat wave, thousands of people fled to air-conditioned theaters to view Al Gore's film about global warming, *An Inconvenient Truth*. The recent sweltering weather heightens fears about the future of our planet.

How hot is it? The first six months of 2006 were the warmest of any year since the United States began keeping records in 1895. For those who live in the South and are more accustomed to the heat, it just seems like the Dog Days of summer.

How hot is it? A friend said, with beads of perspiration flowing down his face, "It's hotter than half of Georgia." He must have meant the half that includes Atlanta, where our daughter lives. She called to report that her beagle had been missing. After a thorough search, she found her pup stretched out in the cool porcelain bathtub as if waiting for someone to turn on the water. Dogs are certainly not the only creatures made uncomfortable by oppressive heat.

So why is this time of the year referred to as Dog Days?

If you can find a place where the night sky is unobscured by artificial lights and pollution, the stars are clearly visible. People of ancient cultures would gaze into the heavens, imagining that they were seeing figures depicted in the stars. It was an ancient version of connect the dots. The configurations that they saw we now call constellations. Amazingly, Native Americans, the ancient Chinese, and the people of Greece and Rome saw similar images in the stars. In these different cultures, separated by oceans, stargazers gave the constellations the same names. Big and Little Bear to Native Americans were Ursa Major and Ursa Minor to Europeans. (Ursa means bear.) We know these constellations best as the Big Dipper and the Little Dipper. Diverse cultures saw in the constellation Taurus, the likeness of a bull, though to Native Americans it was a bison. Canis Major and Canis Minor mean Big Dog and Little Dog.

The brightest star in Canis Major is Sirius, the Dog Star. Sirius was regarded as the companion of the hunter constellation, Orion. The Dog Star is the brightest star in the night sky, so brilliant the Romans thought of it as a secondary sun, providing heat to the earth. In late summer, the Dog Star rises and sets with the sun. Ancient people believed that the conjunction of the sun and the Dog Star was the cause of an extended period of hot muggy weather; hence the name, Dog Days.

We are in the Dog Days of summer. In our part of the world, Dog Days arrive when the hot muggy weather of summer sets in. In the old days it was a time when the pace of life slowed way down, a time when families would go to the mountains. People from the Lowcountry came to the Upstate to resorts like Glenn Springs to escape not only the sultry days of summer, but also the danger of malaria carried by mosquitoes.

Now Dog Days are anything but a period of inactivity. Commercially, we have added a tax-free weekend, which has become one of the busiest times for retail shopping, second only to the days after Thanksgiving. Many schools begin their fall term in the Dog Days of summer. At a time when it is almost too hot to go fishing, we send our children back to school.

Maybe the best way to cope with Dog Days is the old-fashioned way. Back in the days before air conditioning was available, people knew that Dog Days were time to take it easy. Sitting outside after the sun went down, spending the night on a sleeping porch, sipping iced tea in the shade, or soaking in a creek all were ways of coping with the heat. Some kept their perfume in the refrigerator. One man revealed that he put plastic bags of frozen vegetables between his sheets a few minutes before bedtime.

Last weekend, we were returning from a trip to Tennessee. As we traveled through the southern Smoky Mountains near Murphy, North Carolina, we stopped for gasoline at a convenience store. I stood at the counter to pay for a tank of gas and noticed a rough-hewn man in line ahead of me. He purchased two cold beers and requested a plastic cup and a plastic bowl. When I left the store, I caught a glimpse of the man sitting on a rock in the shade of a large sycamore tree. Next to him was a big red dog. The man opened both bottles of beer, pouring one in the cup for himself, the other in the bowl for his dog. As I pumped gasoline into my car, I saw the man finish his beer and the dog lap the bowl dry. Then they both stretched out on the grass beneath the tree for a nap.

Dog Days indeed!

The Ole Swimmin' Hole

On a sweltering afternoon last week, a friend said, "I wish I could go swimming in Barr's Pond back in Lexington County. On a scorching day like today, Barr's pond was the best place to cool off. We'd pile into the bed of a pickup truck. My father would back the truck right up to the water, and we'd all jump out and go swimming."

Many folks have pleasant memories of a favorite swimming hole. A spot in a creek or a pond, large enough and deep enough to swim in, provided blessed relief on a hot summer day.

In a time when there were few swimming pools, the old swimming hole was an important part of my growing-up years. Other than the Camp Croft swimming pool, there were no public places to swim besides rivers and lakes.

In the popular television series *The Beverly Hillbillies*, Jed Clampett and his mountaineer family relocated to Beverly Hills. The family was fascinated by their swimming pool, which they called a cement pond. The Clampetts never seemed to grasp the intended use of the pool. Granny sometimes did the laundry in it and set up her moonshine still next to it.

For the Beverly Hillbillies, the cement pond was a less than acceptable replacement for a mountain swimming hole. So, too, the high-tech pools of our time are just not the same as those natural swimming places that afford such great pleasure.

Some of our best swimming holes were rendered unusable by those whose disregard for clean water turned our waterways into trash dumps. I remember cooling off as a boy in the North Tyger River. By my early adult years, industrial pollution had altered the alkaline content of the river enough to burn human skin. In recent years, environmental efforts to clean up streams and rivers have resulted in cleaner water and healthier places to swim.

Rainbow Lake, north of Boiling Springs, was a popular place to swim. The fancy swimming hole featured a three-story stone tower for diving.

I remember going to Rainbow Lake one hot summer afternoon with my Little League baseball team.

Tommy Stokes, our second baseman, did a headfirst dive off the third story of the tower. Tommy narrowly missed swimmers leaping from the first and second levels as he plummeted into the deep water.

I did my first back-flip off the tower at Rainbow Lake. I made a valiant attempt. I flipped and rotated too far. The back-flip became a painful back-flop.

Soon after I graduated from high school, Rainbow Lake was closed. In 1968, amid the controversy of racial integration, Spartanburg Water Works officials announced that the lake would not reopen for the summer season. A great swimming hole was lost.

When I recall places that I have been swimming, the lakes at scout camp and at Ridgecrest come to mind. What joy!

I have been swimming in the Pigeon River in the Smoky Mountains, Elk Shoals on the North Fork of the New River, and at Burrells' Ford on the Chattooga River. I have enjoyed a refreshing dip in pools at the base of waterfalls like Big Bradley on the Green River and King Creek Falls in Sumter National Forest. Sliding Rock on the Davidson River in Pisgah National Forest is perhaps the coldest swimming hole I have endured.

Safety is always a concern when swimming in a natural setting. Never swim alone! There are no lifeguards. Use the buddy system. Currents can be swift. Rocks can be hazardous. Do not dive! Diving is especially dangerous because the water may be shallow, or there may be hidden rocks below the surface. Slowly wade into the water. Always wear shoes! Broken glass and discarded metal are often present.

One summer Saturday, my parents took us swimming with our cousins at Lake Lure. On Sunday morning, my mother received a telephone call notifying us that a cousin with whom we had been swimming had been stricken with polio. This was before the Salk vaccine had been introduced. All of us were quarantined for the rest of the summer. There was no more swimming that year.

There were two swimming holes I remember most fondly. One was a small pool my friends and I made in a creek behind our house. We dammed up the unnamed stream. A large vine hanging from a poplar tree provided a ready-made swing. With a running start down the hill, we could swing across the creek and back. At the right time we would turn loose, splashing into the muddy pool. The water was a pale yellow. It coated us from neck to toe with a thin layer of mud.

The second place dear to my heart was my grandfather's farm pond.

Skinny-dipping is a well-established tradition at some remote swimming holes. My grandfather's pond was not the place for swimming sans swimsuit!

He built a dock that gave us a perfect launching pad into the cool water. I often fished in this same pond. While swimming, we could feel small bream nibbling our legs.

After we hooked a couple of granddaddy catfish, we didn't even let our feet touch the bottom. Catching a washtub-size snapping turtle made us still more leery. In that same pond, Rudy Mancke and I caught thirty-eight snakes one night. After that, I didn't swim in that pond ever again.

But that's another story.

The Price of a Haircut

When Clare and I lived in Winston-Salem, I won a drawing at a Boy Scout fundraiser. The door prize was a styling at a local hair salon, Delilah's Den. Though I had always gone to a regular barbershop, I decided to try it out since it was free. The resulting haircut was just fine, but Clare quickly informed me that Delilah's Den was forevermore on the black list of places to get a haircut. Delilah the stylist struck her as matching too closely the description of the Biblical Delilah, the one responsible for the downfall of Samson.

Samson had the most expensive haircut on record!

Contrary to the familiar refrain, "Shave and a haircut, two bits," I have never paid less than fifty cents for a haircut.

When I was a freshman at Furman, a senior worked as a barber out of his dormitory room. He charged half a dollar per customer for a cut that conformed to Army standards.

My dad used to give similar haircuts to my three brothers and me. In our garage, using neither comb nor scissors, his only tool was an electric trimmer with a buzz attachment. The resulting hairstyle was just short of bald, allowing our mother to spot a tick at twenty paces.

My first flattop came from Bob Martin when I was in junior high. I used a product called Butch Hair Wax to make the unnatural arrangement stand up. Its effect didn't last long. A flattop and a baseball cap are incompatible.

Nowadays, barbershops are diminishing in number. Salons are replacing many. The folks who actually cut hair are no longer named Bubba or Sarge. They refer to themselves as stylists rather than barbers. They more likely are men with a foreign accent or women named Delilah.

I remember the barbershop as a house of mirrors. Opposing mirrors in front of and behind the row of chairs created an endless series of reflections. The barbershop was a place filled with clouds of cigar smoke mingling with the fragrance of talcum powder and shaving lotion. A barber from my teenage years chewed Redman Tobacco. His brass spittoon would now be considered an antique.

The local barbershop is among the last of the all-male institutions to fade from the American scene. A barber pole and the cigar store Indian were, for years, symbols of welcome refuge for the American male. No more.

The first time I remember a woman entering a barbershop, the intrusion brought a pall of silence settling over the establishment. It was as if we had experienced a close encounter of the third kind.

She was a mama who wanted to be sure the barber treated her none-too-happy son gently and, at the same time, cut the child's hair to suit her.

While she was in the shop, there were no jokes and no fishing stories. There was no banter and no barbershop quarterbacking. The lady did most of the talking.

After the mother and her child departed, a whole lot was said!

Now, if I enter a barbershop where I am known, I am often greeted with, "Hey, Preacher!" followed by the same awkward silence.

After forty-two years as a pastor, I recognize the alarm when it is sounded. Barbers and patrons alike are immediately on guard. Language is sanitized. The best barbershop jokes are censored. It is too high a price to pay for a haircut!

Once I decided to dash into an unfamiliar barbershop for a quick trim while Clare did some shopping.

When I next saw her, she was horrified. "What happened to your hair?"

That was the day I finally lost the privilege of choosing my own barber.

I used to get a haircut at least once every three months whether I needed it or not.

Since Clare started making the decisions about where I am allowed to get my trim, I have a monthly appointment with the same stylist who does her hair. Jeff is a great friend. He gives an excellent haircut. His price is more than fair. Best of all, Jeff is a Green Bay Packers fan who enjoys talking football.

He comes from a line of Georgia barbers. His fine heritage is evidenced by a pair of his uncle's straight razors framed in a shadow box on the wall of his shop. When I visit his place of business, the magazines are Vogue and Cosmopolitan. There is not a *Field and Stream* or *Sports Illustrated* in sight. That is a high price to pay while waiting for a haircut.

Several years ago, while Clare was shopping in historic downtown Inman, I strolled into a barbershop around the corner. The customer in the only barber chair had an Elvis-sized head of hair. The barber worked on the shiny black ducktail while exchanging turkey-hunting stories with the next fellow in line, a man who was almost completely bald.

As the first man paid the usual amount for his haircut, the bald man took his seat in the chair. "Surely, you're not going to charge me the same thing you charged him? I should get a discount!"

The barber responded with a line he must have already used many times. "Yes, you'll get a discount for the haircut, but I'll have to charge you a finder's fee."

Sometimes the price of a haircut is just too high!

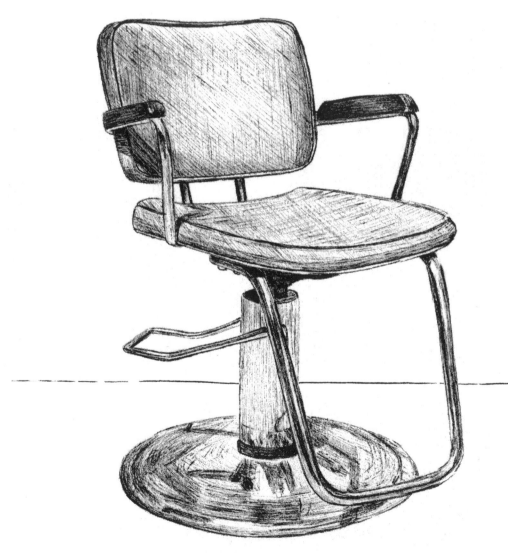

WD-40: The Magic Formula

Clare and I lived in Kentucky during my days as a seminary student. I worked weekends at Lake Cumberland State Boys Camp, an institution for juvenile delinquent young men. I often fished with a friend, Fred, who had previously worked as a commercial fisherman in Florida.

Early in the spring when the white bass were running, Fred and I went night fishing in the deep water of the lake. I was using my favorite rod and reel that had been in storage all winter. Because the reel malfunctioned, I lost the first fish I hooked. Fred said, "Hand me that rig." He disassembled the spinning reel. He produced a can of WD-40 from his tackle box. He sprayed the inner parts of the reel, put the mechanism back together, and handed it to me without a word. I caught my limit of white bass, but, more importantly, I was introduced to the magic of WD-40.

In 1953, three technicians at the San Diego Rocket Chemical Company were assigned the task of inventing a water displacement compound that could be used to lubricate missile parts, prevent rust, and act as a degreaser. The trio of scientists worked tirelessly. The mixture was vital to the fledgling space program of the United States. After thirty-nine failed experiments, the fortieth attempt succeeded. The formula accomplished all of the desired goals. Dubbed Water Displacement Forty, the magic formula came to be known as WD-40.

The Convair Company bought it in bulk to protect the exterior of their Atlas missile. The workers were so pleased with the product, they began smuggling it out to use at home. Executives concluded there just might be a market for it and began to package it in aerosol cans for public consumption. The recipe is carefully guarded, known only to a few people.

Since that night in a boat on Lake Cumberland, I have learned more of the many uses of this remarkable product. Rarely do I need to lubricate missile parts, but I do keep a can of WD-40 near my workbench and another in my barn.

In celebration of their 50th anniversary, the company conducted a survey of its customers to learn their favorite uses of the magic formula. Careful! I can't vouch for any of these, so try them at your own risk.

- Protects silver from tarnishing
- Cleans and lubricates guitar strings
- Lifts oil spots off concrete driveways
- Gives floors that just-waxed sheen without making them slippery
- Repels flies from cows
- Restores and cleans chalkboards
- Removes lipstick stains
- Loosens stubborn zippers
- Untangles jewelry chains
- Spruces up stainless steel sinks
- Cleans grease and grime from the barbecue grill
- Prevents ceramic and terra cotta garden pots from oxidizing
- Removes tomato stains from clothing
- Eliminates water spots from glass shower doors
- Camouflages scratches in ceramic and marble floors
- Keeps scissors working smoothly
- Silences squeaky door hinges
- Insures a super-fast descent on a children's sliding board
- Lubricates gearshift and deck lever on riding mowers
- Rids rocking chairs and swings of creaking
- Unsticks stuck windows
- Makes an umbrella easier to open and close
- Polishes dashboards and vinyl bumpers
- Stops squeaks in electric fans
- Lubricates wheel sprockets on tricycles, wagons, and bicycles
- Quiets noisy fan belts
- Prevents rust from forming on saws and other tools
- Removes splattered grease on stove
- Defogs the bathroom mirror
- Lubricates prosthetic limbs
- Discourages pigeons from perching on the balcony
- Removes all traces of duct tape
- Cleans bugs off of automobile bumpers and grills

WD-40 has been designated as the official multipurpose problem solver of NASCAR, the National Association for Stock Car Auto Racing. Some folks have even tried spraying it on their arms, hands, and knees to relieve arthritis pain. A few anglers claim that applying it to their lures attracts fish. A bus driver in Southeast Asia reported using the lubricant to dislodge a python that had coiled himself around the undercarriage of the bus. WD-40 is used to keep the bolts on the Golden Gate Bridge rust free and to protect the Statue of Liberty from the elements.

Last month a friend who has spent most of his life as an automobile mechanic was hospitalized in the Heart Center at Spartanburg Regional Medical Center. Several years ago he had surgery to replace a valve in his heart. The mechanical valve worked well until recently.

After discussing several treatment options with his physician, he suggested, "Couldn't you just install a grease fitting on my chest and squirt a little WD-40 on that valve in there?"

Might be worth a try.

A Big Fish Story

My cousin recently returned from a fishing trip with several of his buddies. The group returned with two large coolers filled with striped bass. I enjoyed sharing the moment as he bragged about the day's catch. Everybody on the trip reeled in his limit of the large fish. "We just wore them out!" he said.

The striped bass, sometimes called a rockfish, is a saltwater fish found along the East Coast from Maine to Florida. It's also the state fish of South Carolina. An avid angler from Georgia caught the South Carolina record in 2002. His fifty-nine-pound, eight-ounce rockfish was landed at Lake Hartwell.

Stripers, by nature, migrate from saltwater up freshwater rivers to spawn. Before the Army Corps of Engineers constructed dams on our major rivers, striped bass would swim from the ocean into the Santee-Cooper River system. When the dams were built, some of the large stripers became landlocked rockfish, an unfortunate oxymoron for any fish. Eventually, large impoundments like Lake Moultrie, Lake Marion, Lake Murray, and Lake Hartwell were stocked with striped bass. The fish have become acclimatized to freshwater.

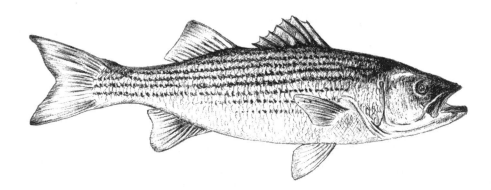

Listening to my cousin, I reflected on a day in mid-June several years ago. Three friends and I left early in the morning to go to Lake Murray. Striper fishing was our agenda for the day. The lake was calm. The sun was hot. Fishing was slow. By lunchtime, we had only one striper in the boat. We fished through the afternoon. The sun was blazing down. On the sonar device in the boat we saw an indication of fish, but the striped bass would not bite.

At about 5 p.m., the man who owned the boat said, "Maybe we ought to just call it a day."

The wind had picked up. The water was choppy. Fish sometimes become more active in rough water than in calm water. I asked if we could try one more place.

Next to one of the islands in the big water of Lake Murray, the bottom drops quickly to a depth of ninety feet. As we moved over that area of the lake, echoes on the sonar indicted large fish right on the bottom. I reached in the bait well. I got the largest gizzard shad I could find, put him on my hook, and dropped my line to the bottom. I placed the fishing rod in a rod holder. Just as I did, the rod tip bent down beneath the water, and curved back under the boat. I grabbed the rod and set the hook as hard as I could. The fiberglass rod broke in half above the last metal rod guide.

I watched as the end of the rod slid down the line toward the water. I might as well have been fishing with a broom handle. The fish on the other end made a run, pulling line off the reel. With that distinctive hum so thrilling to a fisherman, the fish continued its run until I could see bare reel. I knew I had to turn his head. I gave one quick jerk on the fishing rod. The fish stopped. We moved the boat to the fish, and as we did, I took in line. When we were above the fish, I worked him up from the bottom of the lake. Slowly, he came closer and closer to the surface. The striper ran again, this time not so far.

Because the rod was broken, I could not feel the fish. I knew he was large. My arms and back were aching from the extended fight. When I finally saw the fish on the surface of the water, I could hardly believe my eyes. I reeled him to the boat; one of my friends netted him and brought him aboard. It was the largest freshwater fish I have ever caught—a twenty-three-pound striped bass.

My cousin said of his striper fishing, "We wore them out!" I would reverse that in sharing my own striper story. "He wore me out!"

I had my picture made with my prized striped bass. When my uncle saw the photograph, he quipped, "Whoever caught that fish was lying."

The Gray Man

During the recent visit to the Carolinas by tropical storm Ernesto, multitudes of beach lovers, especially those planning a Labor Day trip to the coast, watched weather reports with concern. I was reminded of my favorite places along the ocean, retreats where my family and I have enjoyed vacations. The storm also brought to mind the story of a benevolent ghost from Pawley's Island.

Do you believe in ghosts? Many people in the Georgetown area of South Carolina do. If you ask about ghosts in that part of the country, you are likely to hear the story of the Gray Man of Pawley's Island.

Years ago, before the Civil War, Pawley's Island was a place where rice planters kept summer homes. The plantation owners would go to the small island across the marsh to get away from the oppressive temperatures and the voracious mosquitoes that were a fact of life in humid, Lowcountry summers. The ocean breezes and the solitude of the island were a respite from heat and malaria.

In one of these summer homes, there lived a beautiful young girl. She had a suitor named Beauregard who had been away in Europe for several months. Finally, she got word that her true love was sailing home. She decorated the house on Pawley's Island with greenery and flowers and asked her mother to prepare his favorite meals.

When Beauregard arrived, it was a happy occasion for the entire family. In the midst of their celebration, Beauregard challenged one of the servants to a horse race down the beach. The race was on! About halfway down the beach, Beauregard took a shortcut through a marshy area. His horse suddenly stumbled, throwing him from his saddle into quicksand. Beauregard was unable to free himself. The servant watched helplessly as the young man sank to his death.

The young woman was grief-stricken at the loss of her sweetheart. She wept for days. Every morning she wandered the beach alone as if she were expecting the man she loved to return.

One morning, a great distance down the beach, she saw a man. He was dressed entirely in gray, standing on top of a sand dune, gazing across the water. As the young woman moved closer, her heart began to pound. The man seemed to resemble Beauregard. As she got closer, a gray mist came up from the ocean, swirled around him, and he vanished from her sight.

That night, she had a disturbing nightmare about an ocean storm. In her dream, she saw Beauregard dressed in gray, beckoning her. The following morning, she shared the dream with her family. She also told them of the strange encounter on the beach the day before. They became quite alarmed. Her father insisted that they take her immediately to visit a physician in Charleston. The entire family accompanied the young woman.

While the family was in Charleston, a hurricane roared across the island, destroying everything. When the young woman and her family learned of the devastation on Pawley's Island, she realized that the appearance of the Gray Man had saved their lives. She was convinced that he was the ghost of Beauregard!

In those days, long before the advent of Doppler Radar and weather satellites, tropical storms and hurricanes struck suddenly and without warning. Like the grieving young woman, many others since have believed that the Gray Man was their protector.

To this day, the residents of Pawley's Island declare that the Gray Man is in their midst. He resides, they say, at the Pelican Inn, one of the oldest structures on the island. The islanders tell of times when the Gray Man appeared to signal an approaching storm. The apparition is said to have warned numerous residents just before Hurricane Hazel arrived in 1953. All were evacuated, and no lives were lost.

Pawley's Island Chapel is a small structure built out into the marsh on stilts. Several times, while our family is at Pawley's on vacation, I have been invited to lead worship in the chapel. On one occasion, I shared the tale of the Gray Man. In my sermon, I made the connection with a story from the Gospel of Matthew. The disciples were in a fishing boat on the Sea of Galilee. Throughout the night, the disciples, most of whom were seasoned fishermen, rode out a fierce storm. As morning approached, they saw a figure walking toward them across the waves.

They were terrified and cried out in fear. "It is a ghost!"

Then, their master spoke to them, "Take courage! Don't be afraid!"

Several days after I had delivered the sermon, I was walking along the beach. It was dusk. A band of thunderstorms had passed and moved out to sea. As the sun set over the marsh with pink, purple, and orange swirls, the sky over the ocean was dark. Flashes of lightning punctuated the clouds.

Following the storm, the evening air was cool, and the breeze was brisk. Few other people were on the beach, but I noticed a couple walking toward me. As we passed each other in the fading light, they recognized that I was the preacher from the chapel service the previous Sunday morning.

"You had us worried for a moment," the woman said.

The man added, "I knew you weren't Jesus, but, for a moment, we wondered if you might be the Gray Man."

The Gray Man? Me?

Well, at least he is a kind and helpful ghost!

The Many Uses of Duct Tape

The bride-to-be was worried and fretful about the details of her wedding. To ease her anxiety, she ate ravenously for several days prior to the marriage. When the big day arrived, she took her wedding gown, ordered and fitted months before, to the church. Just two hours before the wedding, she discovered that she could not fit into her dress. Panic ensued!

The father of the bride kept a tool box in the trunk of his car. Eureka! Buried under the jumbled contents was a roll of duct tape. Wrapping the silver adhesive around his daughter's midsection, he fashioned a makeshift corset, binding up the bride so she could wear the gown.

"My daddy knew just what to do!" exclaimed the happy bride as she ate her second piece of wedding cake. "My dress fit perfectly!"

Duct tape, developed during World War II, was originally named Duck Tape. Used as a waterproof sealing tape for ammunition cases, the versatile product was also used to repair military equipment, including jeeps, guns, and aircraft.

Postwar, the United States experienced a boom in the housing industry. The name duct tape evolved because of its application in heating and air conditioning installation. Duct tape sealed the air ducts.

Its value is evidenced by its presence in most tool boxes. A friend contends that a handyman needs two indispensable tools: duct tape for sticking things and WD-40 for un-sticking things.

Wikipedia, the online encyclopedia, reports that Duck Products, a manufacturer of duct tape, produces the adhesive in a wide range of colors. The company annually sponsors a competition that offers a college scholarship to the high school student who creates the most stylish formal prom wear made from duct tape.

A previous competition of Duck Products was called Stuck in

Traffic. Vehicles decorated with creative duct tape designs were judged and prizes were awarded.

Some people enjoy making novelty items out of the adhesive. At a recent youth group function at our church, I noticed a teenager sporting a duct tape purse! She had crafted the bag from her dad's handy roll.

I have since learned that designer duct tape accessories are available for purchase. Love My Bag, known for retailing major name brand fashion designers such as Prada and Fendi, has begun retailing an exclusive line of duct tape handbags from the designer Vanessa Jean. Browsing her website reveals sixteen different handbag creations available in a riot of colors, all very affordable at less than fifty dollars.

A medical study that was announced on a major news network stated that an application of duct tape can be used as an effective treatment for warts. The procedure even has a name—duct tape occlusion therapy! Please consult your physician before trying this method of wart removal.

The Duct Tape Guys, Jim Berg and Tim Nyberg, have written seven books about the many uses of duct tape. Their best selling books have sold over 1.5 million copies. They coined the motto, "It ain't broke; it just needs duct tape." Their website features thousands of duct tape uses contributed from people around the world. Here is a sampling:

"The paint on my car was peeling, so I redid my entire car in duct tape," reads an entry.

A teenager wrote, "I have an artificial leg, and out of pure stupidity, I broke it at the ankle. After about two hours of worrying about what my

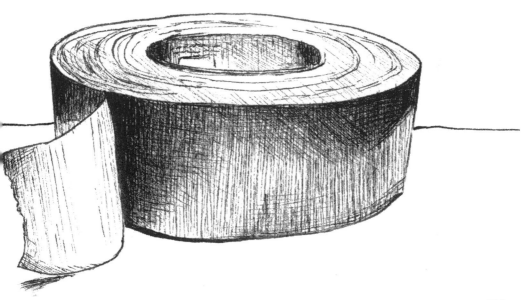

parents would say, I wrapped it with duct tape and walked on it for nearly two weeks."

A high school student entered, "I'm in the marching band, and I broke my trumpet. We have no band budget, so we duct-taped the horn back together."

From an avid hunter, "My deer stand broke, so I duct taped myself in the tree!"

The troubled space flight of Apollo 13 has been chronicled in a movie starring Tom Hanks. A real-life drama in space began with the unforgettable words, radioed back to earth by Jack Swigert, "Houston, we've had a problem here!"

En route to the moon, the command module was shaken by an explosion. The crew evacuated the space capsule and entered the attached lunar landing module, using it as a lifeboat. The square carbon dioxide filters from Apollo 13's failed command module had to be modified to fit round receptacles in the lunar landing module. The challenge was the proverbial problem—how to fit a square peg into a round hole. Without the modification, the three astronauts would have perished in space.

On the ground in Houston, Ed Smylie, chief of NASA mission control engineers, designed the modification using duct tape. Following the directions relayed from Houston, the Apollo 13 crew made the repairs using their own roll of duct tape. The filters started working, saving the lives of the three astronauts onboard. Later, Ed said that he knew the problem was solvable when the crew confirmed that duct tape was on board the spacecraft.

"I felt like we were home free," Ed Smylie, a native of Mississippi, quipped. "One thing a Southern boy will never say is 'I don't think duct tape will fix that.'"

Among the nicknames for duct tape is "Jesus Tape," derived from the miraculous properties of the silver adhesive. To some the nickname may seem sacrilegious. Apollo 13 astronauts Jim Lovell, Jack Swigert, and Fred Haise may disagree. Duct tape saved their lives!

The Hazards of Cell Phones

The invention of the telephone revolutionized human communication. On Valentine's Day, February 14, 1876, two men filed separately for the patent on the telephone at the New York patent office.

A Scotsman, Alexander Graham Bell, applied for a patent just two hours ahead of American Elisha Gray. Both men had been working on the invention, but Gray had difficulty mastering the transmitter. Bell worked tirelessly even while Gray became discouraged.

According to the famous story, the first intelligible conversation by telephone occurred March 6, 1876. Alexander Graham Bell rang up his assistant, Thomas Watson. "Come here, Watson. I want you."

Dr. Martin Cooper, an engineer for Motorola, invented the first cell phone. On April 3, 1973, Dr. Cooper made the first cellular phone call. More than one billion people now use cellular phones worldwide. In China, India, and other Asian countries, the cell phone industry is growing rapidly.

Technology is supposed to make our lives easier. Maybe you have discovered, as I have, that there are times when high-tech gadgets create confusion. My experiences with cell phones provide good examples.

The church that I serve provides a cell phone to assist me in my pastoral work. I sometimes refer to my cell phone as my leash. It is the way the church office and my family keep up with me.

About three years ago, I was at home on a Friday afternoon, working on Sunday's sermon and making calls on my cell phone. It was a cold, rainy day. I had a fever and a splitting headache. One of our tried-and-true headache remedies is a hot neck wrap. It is a flannel bag filled with cherry pits. When heated in the microwave oven, the hot wrap brings soothing relief.

That afternoon, I was using the neck wrap at the same time I was making calls on the cell phone. After a time, the warm wrap lost its heat and its effectiveness. I folded the wrap and placed it back in the microwave for reheating. No sooner had I set the microwave for two minutes than

I realized I no longer had my cell phone. I had searched only for a moment, when suddenly, I noticed that the microwave oven was emitting an offensive odor.

You guessed it! In my fevered state, I had enfolded the cell phone into the neck wrap. As you might imagine, the cell phone melted, the neck wrap was ruined, and my headache was worse. Within a few months, the microwave had to be replaced as well. So much for the convenience of high-tech gizmos.

Cell phones today are equipped with a choice of ringer sounds. I have heard "Dixie," "The Yellow Rose of Texas," Bach, rock, and rap blaring from cell phones. Sermons, board meetings, and many a sound sleep have been disturbed by the jangling tones of cell phones.

Recently I was in a meeting with a dozen or more college students. A cell phone interrupted with Scott Joplin's "Maple Leaf Rag." Within two minutes, another mobile phone issued forth with the same Joplin piano tune. The coincidence of the same tune coming from two different cell phones prompted a spontaneous survey. No fewer than four of the students had their phones programmed to "Maple Leaf Rag."

When I make hospital visits, my habit is to wash my hands between visits and then again as I leave the hospital. Last week, on my way out of Spartanburg Regional Medical Center, I stopped in the men's room on the first floor. As I entered the door and turned on the water at the sink, a voice from one of the stalls asked, "How are you doing?"

"Just fine," I said, knowing that sometimes people recognize me in unusual places when I do not recognize them.

"What have you been up to?" he said.

"I've been making hospital visits," I answered. "We have several church members here. One who had surgery early this morning."

"Can you call me right back?" said the voice from inside the stall. "Some guy just walked in. He must be a preacher, and he thinks I'm talking to him."

I dried my hands and left quickly. On my way out I was almost sure I heard the strains of "Maple Leaf Rag."

By the way, I have it on good authority: there will be no telephones in heaven.

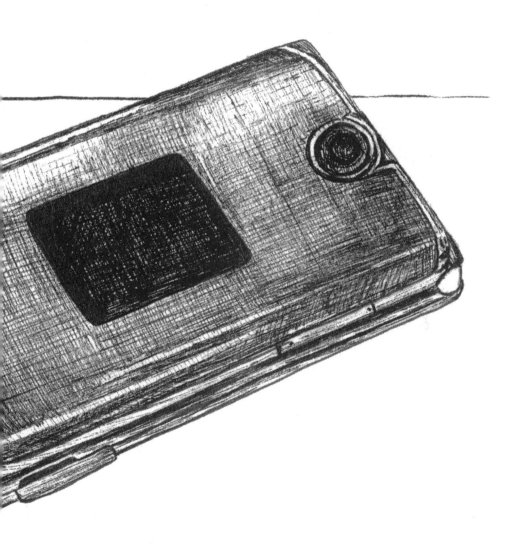

Coping with Drought

Miss Maude and Creech lived in an unpainted clapboard house in Barnwell County, South Carolina. The house was perched atop heart pine logs. The house had no running water. The bathroom was an outhouse at the end of a path that passed a beautiful flower garden. Miss Maude and her husband, known only by his last name, Creech, enjoyed a simple life. Their home was lighted with kerosene lamps. They cooked on a wood stove, which also served as their source of heat. In the summertime, they would sit together in matching rocking chairs on a shaded porch that wrapped around the house.

Miss Maude wore a sunbonnet and a faded calico dress. She cooled herself with a fan woven from a palmetto palm. Creech wore a straw hat, a long-sleeved cotton shirt, and overalls. They drew water from a well.

They each took a bath once a week, usually on Saturday, whether they needed it or not. They took turns bathing in a galvanized tin tub in the kitchen. Miss Maude washed dishes in a blue enamel pan. The water left over from washing was taken to the garden. It was poured from a white porcelain pitcher around individual plants, providing the moisture needed in the Lowcountry heat.

Their lifestyle was simple. Their flower garden was beautiful. Their vegetable garden was fruitful. Their conservation of water is to be admired and emulated.

The Spartanburg *Herald-Journal* reported that the month of August 2007 set records for high temperatures and low rainfall. The state and local representatives from the Drought Response Committee reported September 5, 2007 that conditions have continued to deteriorate. The committee upgraded the drought level to severe for all counties in South Carolina except Beaufort and Jasper.

According to Hope Mizzell, state climatologist, the drought impact to agriculture, forestry, and water levels indicates an extreme drought for much of the Upstate.

In July and August, the South Carolina Forestry Commission responded to 518 wildfires that burned more than 2,730 acres. The high temperatures made it hard for firefighters. Without widespread rainfall, the fall wildfire season has the potential to be severe.

State Hydrologist Bud Badr reported all lake levels are below normal except Lake Murray. Fifteen water systems have imposed water restrictions.

The *Herald-Journal* carried an article by Janet S. Spencer about the problem in one rural Upstate community. Wells are drying up in Rock Springs in Cherokee County. Confronted with a lack of potable drinking water, about 110 residents of the community off Highway 18 north of Blacksburg are rationing to conserve the scant supply of water. Residents have been advised not to drink the water.

Coping with the declining water table is difficult. One resident said, "Many have to space out use of their water for washing clothes during the day, bathing at night. One family built a homemade holding tank with a timer on the well pump. It runs at intervals and fills up at night. That usually gets them through the next day."

Digging new wells is not always a solution. Some attempts to find a better source of water end in disappointment with only a deep, dry hole. "Rock Springs has gone from desperate for water, to critical, to begging," said one man who has always lived in the area.

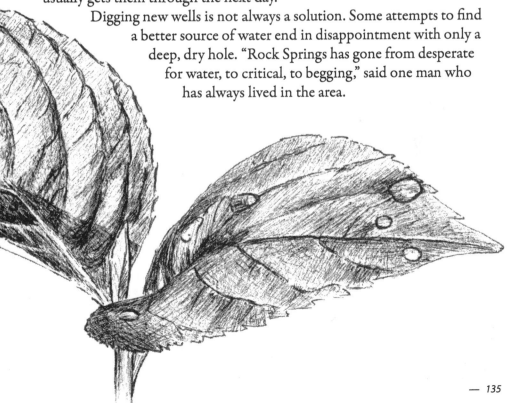

Though the situation is not nearly so critical for most of us, the drought that has persisted in the southeastern United States through the summer has been difficult for many of us who love to garden. We have tried to stay ahead of the drought by watering regularly and by mulching deeply.

This summer the drought has been so severe that many gardeners have lost prized trees and shrubs. Vegetable gardens and flower gardens have suffered. I have paid special attention to the plants in my garden that have survived. Some have done well and have flourished even through this hot, dry summer.

While I have lost a number of plants, I have learned what to plant next year and what not to plant. Next year there will be more succulents like the always-reliable sedums; more heat tolerant annuals such as vinca, cosmos, cleome, and portulaca; and more drought-tolerant perennials— verbena, black-eyed Susans, yarrow, and coneflowers. Even the miniature roses have survived the drought well.

Clare and I have also learned some important lessons about conserving water. It is not wise to leave a sprinkler running for several hours. It is impractical because of the loss of water due to evaporation.

Plastic pans in our kitchen sink conserve dishwater. Hanging baskets, flowerpots, and flower boxes all get a daily drink of this recycled water. Shorter showers are in order. A three-gallon bucket placed in the shower conserves the water we waste until we get the right temperature. Trees and shrubs that must be watered deeply love this recycled water.

We've learned from necessity the lessons that Miss Maude and Creech demonstrated so beautifully on their farm long ago.

Coping with the drought requires that we all conserve as much as possible. Pray for communities like the people of Rock Springs. Most of all, pray for rain.

The Versatile Shrimp

Here is a riddle. What has twenty legs, swims forward and backwards, and glows in the dark? The United States Synchronized Swimming Team! Why do they glow in the dark? Since 1984, they have won more gold and silver medals than any other US Olympic team.

Actually, the answer to the riddle is a shrimp.

In the movie Forrest Gump, Bubba explains the value of shrimp to Forrest: "Shrimp is the fruit of the sea. You can barbecue it, boil it, broil it, bake it, sauté it. You have shrimp-kabobs, shrimp Creole, shrimp gumbo. Pan fried, deep fried, stir-fried. There's pineapple shrimp, lemon shrimp, coconut shrimp, pepper shrimp, shrimp soup, shrimp stew, shrimp salad, shrimp and potatoes, shrimp burger, shrimp sandwich. That's about it."

While Bubba left out several shrimp dishes, his list showcases the versatility of shrimp. The tasty crustaceans, first cousins to lobsters and crabs, are South Carolina's most valuable seafood crop.

Shallow-water shrimp in South Carolina come in three colors: white, brown, and pink. Similar in taste, the three species also have similar life cycles. However, they mature and spawn at different times of year. They are prolific little critters. A single female may spawn several times and produce up to one million eggs.

White shrimp account for about two-thirds of the state's catch.

Small fishing communities, scattered along South Carolina's coast, depend heavily on the annual shrimp harvest. The shrimping industry also makes a significant impact on the economy of Mount Pleasant, Beaufort, and Hilton Head.

The peak of the shrimp season runs from July through October. The large five-ton trawlers are restricted to offshore areas for most of the seven-month shrimp season. In late summer and fall, when the shrimp are of marketable size, the inshore sections of bays and sounds are opened for trawling. Small-boat operators generally do inshore shrimping.

Shrimping is a part of the spirit and the mystique of the sea. As we sit on the deck of a beach house looking out at the ocean, we see near the horizon a trawler dragging double nets. Followed by hordes of seagulls picking up the leftovers, the shrimp boat is a picture of tranquility. While enjoying a shrimp cocktail at a creekside seafood restaurant, we gaze at shrimp boats resting in calm waters. These images are delightful but deceptive.

Last week, Clare and I were at Pawley's Island. We enjoyed shrimp and grits at a café in Georgetown where the local folks gather. A tired, grizzled fellow took a table near us, and we struck up a conversation. He was a shrimp boat captain who told me about his work.

Traditionally a family business, shrimping is a demanding enterprise. Successful shrimp boat captains know the coastal waters like most people know their backyards. They can accurately predict and locate the site of the best catch in varying wind, weather, and tide conditions.

During the shrimp season, the shrimper gets up early and puts in a long day. The crew arrives at the dock at 4 a.m., and the trawler is soon heading out on the ocean. The captain maneuvers the boat toward the shrimping grounds, usually within six miles of shore.

Most shrimp trawlers are diesel-powered and double-rigged, towing two nets simultaneously through rich, offshore waters. Trawlers scoop up more than shrimp. Many other bottom-dwelling creatures become part of their catch. Shrimpers refer to the unwanted species as trash fish. These

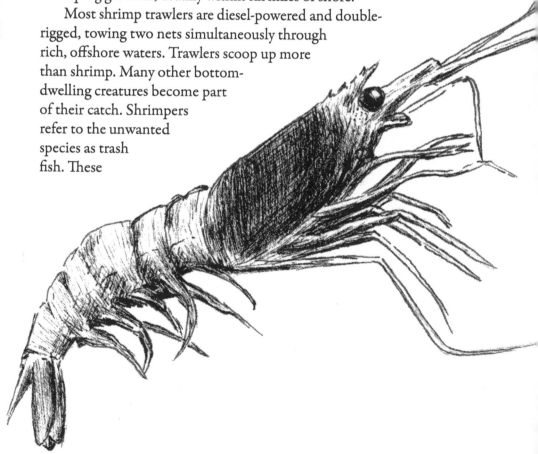

include crabs, jellyfish, and turtles. As soon as the nets are emptied on deck, the live trash catch is thrown overboard. However, some shrimpers keep fish like flounder, spot, and mackerel that bring a good market price.

After one or more days at sea, captain and crew return to port with their catch. At the dock, the work is far from finished. Tasks include unloading, sorting, and packing the shrimp in ice. While some shrimp are sold at the dock or in local seafood markets, most South Carolina shrimp are shipped out of our state.

Our family looks forward to an annual week at the beach. We invite all of our children, as many as can come for as long as they can stay. The children always request one or more meals of cold boiled shrimp. I buy several pounds of fresh local shrimp. I boil them and serve them on ice with several choices of sauce. Each family member peels and dips until they have had their fill. The remaining shrimp become fair game the next day.

While we were at Pawley's Island last week, I was fishing in the surf. A friend had said that blue fish and spot tails were in close and hitting hard. I was using shrimp for bait, of course. I did have several hard strikes but no fish to show for it. Something pesky kept eating my bait. I was hoping for a blue fish and I finally landed a catch. He was blue alright—a blue crab. Clare came near to ask the question no fisherman wants to hear when there is nothing in the bucket.

"Have you caught anything?"

"No," I said. "Crabs keep eating my shrimp."

"Smart crabs," she quipped.

I put away my fishing gear, cleaned up, and took my wife out to dinner. Like the smart blue crabs, we both had shrimp.

Mama's Candy Apples

When I was a boy, back in the days before the Grinch stole Halloween, October 31st was one of the most anticipated evenings of the year. All Hallow's Eve was second only to Christmas Eve when excitement, for kids, permeated the night air. No sooner had the sun gone down than costumed kids of every age flooded the streets of the neighborhood, knocking on doors and shouting "Trick-or-treat!"

Parents escorting their children stood a few yards away, guardian angels watching over small gremlins and goblins. The trick-or-treaters carried plastic jack-o-lanterns or paper bags to collect their bounty.

My friend Rusty always dressed as a pirate, carrying a large pillowcase to stash his booty. He folded a second pillowcase in his pocket, just in case the first one reached capacity. Rusty's Halloween range was far greater than mine. He worked his neighborhood of Ben Avon before dark, and then came to my street about the time I walked out of my house dressed as a hobo.

We ventured from one house to the next collecting treats. Rusty carried a spray can of whipping cream as he made his rounds. If the treat at a home was particularly generous, Rusty marked the driveway with a whipped cream star. A full-sized candy bar— Hershey, Snickers, Milky Way, or Three Musketeers—merited a star.

I learned a lot from Rusty. His advice was to avoid large groups. Two beggars at a time are enough for any home. Five or six together usually get smaller gifts.

Occasionally we would have meetings with other trick-or-treaters to discuss where the best handouts were. Rusty was like a crafty angler concealing his best fishing hole. He never told about the houses with the whipped cream star. On the other hand, he gathered as much information as he could.

Sometimes Rusty would trade treats with other consultants. He always came out on the better end of the deal. I saw him trade three packs of Juicy Fruit Chewing Gum for a Hershey Chocolate Almond bar and a pack of Topps Baseball cards. The pack of baseball cards had both a Mickey Mantle and a Willie Mays card inside.

One dark night, at one of the roadside conferences, an unlikely clown revealed that there was "a drunk guy on the other side of Duncan Park Lake

giving away silver dollars."

After the meeting broke up, Rusty said, "Let's go!"

I knew he meant to the other side of the lake, but the trip was beyond my range and would have taken me long past my curfew. We walked back toward my house.

Rusty stopped at a driveway with a whipped cream star. He took off his pirate's eye patch, removed the bandana from his head, walked to the door, and collected a second Three Musketeers bar from the same house. He added a second whipped cream star to mark the driveway.

"I'll see you later," he said as he left for the other side of Duncan Park Lake.

I went home.

My mother knew how to throw a party. She believed every holiday deserved to be celebrated to the fullest. St. Valentine and St. Patrick got almost as much attention as St. Nicholas.

Halloween was one of her favorites. Orange pumpkins adorned the front porch. Inside our home glowing jack-o-lanterns and gossamer ghosts were everywhere.

Mama's contribution to trick-or-treaters was a candy apple, the treat everybody wanted most of all. Mama dipped apples, each fitted with a short, sharpened stick, into a hot candy coating. If you have ever burned your hands with a hot glue gun, you know what dipping a candy apple is like.

Every Halloween, Mama made hundreds. Children came trick-or-treating at our house from all over.

Mama bought apples by the case at Community Cash grocery store. The family took turns at a pencil sharpener putting points on the dowel rods Dad had cut at the lumberyard. The apples were washed, and the sticks inserted before Mama cooked the candy.

My sister, Beth, now the queen of candy apples in our family, was willing to share Mama's recipe. She said the technique for making the treat can be tricky.

The candy ingredients are:

2 cups sugar
1 package cinnamon drops (Mama stockpiled these.)
1 tablespoon red food coloring
1 cup water
1 teaspoon vinegar

Mama's directions were: Cook to 265 degrees, somewhere between soft and "hard crack" stage on a candy thermometer. Dip apples. Place on marble slab greased with real butter. Wrap in plastic bags when cool. One recipe makes twelve to twenty-four candy apples.

Mama made hundreds of candy apples every Halloween.

Several years ago, I conducted a funeral service for a man who grew up in our neighborhood. Following the funeral, the brother of the deceased remembered fondly coming to our house on Halloween. He said that Mama always invited the children into her kitchen to see their costumes.

"We would get a candy apple, go home, change disguises, and come back for another." Then he made a confession. "One year, my brother and I came trick-or-treating at your house four times. We got four candy apples!" Then he added, "Your mother knew. She called us by name and said, 'You boys have been here four times. I think that's enough this year.'"

"What made you think you could get away with that?" I asked.

He grinned, "There were four whipped cream stars by your driveway."

Of Grape Juice and Bourbon Whiskey

I went to seminary in Louisville, Kentucky. At the time, the Ohio River city was known as the home of seven seminaries and seven distilleries. I probably missed about half of what Louisville had to offer.

Being a tee-totaler, I am certainly no authority on alcoholic beverages. When it comes to mixed drinks, iced tea with a shot of pineapple juice is about my limit.

I read a review of a Washington, D.C., restaurant in an upscale magazine. The food editor touted a new cocktail, Grape and Grain. It is a mixture of grape juice, Kentucky Bourbon, and orange bitters. It brought to my mind the stories of two men.

Thomas Welch immigrated to the United States in 1834 as a boy. He graduated from medical college and became a physician. After practicing for only two years, his declining health led him to establish a successful dentistry practice in Vineland, New Jersey.

When Welch came to Vineland, the town was a temperance stronghold. Even so, no less than a dozen places sold liquor. Welch was a staunch Prohibitionist who actively worked to end the sale of alcoholic beverages in New Jersey.

Welch was so adamant in his convictions about alcohol that he wanted churches to discontinue the use of wine in communion services. He originated a method of preserving grape juice. He called his product Dr. Welch's Unfermented Wine.

Typically, purple grape juice is made from Concord grapes. It is commonly used by Christian denominations opposed to the use of alcoholic beverages in the observance of the Lord's Supper.

Bourbon is an American whiskey named for Bourbon County,

Kentucky. It is made primarily of corn. It is aged in new, charred-oak barrels, usually for at least four years.

Bourbon can be made anywhere in the United States that it is legal to distill spirits. Currently all but a few brands are made in the Commonwealth of Kentucky.

Fort Harrod, an early outpost in Bourbon County, Kentucky, was established in 1774. The settlers planted corn. When their harvests exceeded what they and their livestock could eat, they converted the surplus into whiskey.

Named after the French royal family, Bourbon County covered a large area noted for its limestone spring water. Even after the region was divided into smaller counties, it continued to be known as Old Bourbon. Located within Old Bourbon was the principal Ohio River port from which whiskey was exported. Old Bourbon was stenciled on the barrels to indicate their port of origin. Old Bourbon whiskey was the first corn liquor most people had ever tasted.

Each county in Kentucky names a favorite son as the inventor of Bourbon whiskey. There was no single inventor of the product. Jim Beam, James Crow, Evan Williams, James Pepper, Edmund Taylor, William Weller, and the Wathen Family were among the earlier Bourbon makers in the Bluegrass State.

Tennessee whiskey is similar to Kentucky Bourbon, in that it is made of corn mash and is aged in new, charred-oak barrels, typically for four or more years. Unlike Bourbon, Tennessee whiskey is filtered through a thick layer of maple charcoal before it is put into casks for aging. This step gives the whiskey a distinctive flavor. Jack Daniel's and George Dickel were the two most prominent makers of Tennessee whiskey.

While no single person can really claim the distinction of inventing Bourbon whiskey, the credit is often given to Elijah Craig. He was born in Orange County, Virginia, in 1738. Following a brief sojourn in South Carolina, he crossed the Appalachian Mountains to settle in Kentucky about the time the Declaration of Independence was signed. Craig was a shrewd businessman. He built Kentucky's first paper mill. In 1789, he founded a distillery in Georgetown, Kentucky. Craig's distillery was the first to age corn whiskey in new, charred-oak barrels. This innovation was the decisive step in turning moonshine into Bourbon whiskey.

Welch and Craig have something in common that is surprising.

Thomas Welch graduated from Wesleyan Seminary. At the age of nineteen, he entered the gospel ministry. He was ordained in the Wesleyan Methodist Church, serving a church near New York City. He continued in the ministry until his voice failed him. It was then that he entered medical school. He is remembered for the grape juice he developed and the company he founded, Welch's Grape Juice.

Elijah Craig, said to have been the inventor of Bourbon whiskey, was ordained a Baptist minister in 1771. He was imprisoned briefly in South Carolina, apparently for disturbing the peace with his sermons. He then moved to Bourbon County and settled near Frankfort, Kentucky. In 1777, he became pastor of Blue Run Church. His distillery, Heaven Hill, produces a brand of Bourbon named Elijah Craig. The whiskey is considered to be one of the firm's premium products.

Grape and Grain, a mixture of grape juice and Kentucky Bourbon, is a concoction derived from the labors of two ministers, a tee-totaling Methodist and an imbibing Baptist.

Go figure!

The Price of a Postage Stamp

I stopped by the post office to mail packages to our out-of-town children and grandchildren. As I waited in line, I overheard a conversation between a postal clerk and a customer. The woman was in line to purchase just one stamp. She complained, "I have so many stamps at home, but I never seem to have one when I need it. Just last week I bought a roll of one hundred stamps, and here I am without one."

The clerk responded, "You need to use up those thirty-seven cent stamps. The price is going up after the first of the year."

That transaction completed, the clerk slid a "Next Window Please" sign in place and announced, "I'm going to lunch."

Three of us were left standing in line to wait our turn for the one window remaining open. The man behind me commented, "No wonder rates are going up. Customer service gets more expensive by the day."

The same day, our church secretary lamented, "Some of our members received their weekly newsletters two days later than normal. I don't understand. I mailed them the same as usual."

I recounted the exchange I had witnessed in the post office earlier, including the fact that postal rates were going to increase.

A deacon who happened to be in the office quipped, "The post office has to increase rates. We have to pay the storage fee so they can keep those newsletters two extra days."

Unused stamps of various denominations are tucked away throughout our home. Clare and I have recently made an effort to use all of the leftover stamps we could find. Some we unearthed went back to the time when first class postage was twenty-nine cents and stamps still had to be licked. We purchased enough one-, two-, and five-cent stamps to complete the postage needed to use up all our old stamps.

Some recipients of our mailings might have guessed our plan. An envelope with a twenty-nine-cent Hank Williams bracketed by a five-cent toleware coffee pot, a two-cent Navajo silver necklace, and a one-cent ring-necked pheasant would certainly be noticed. One might conclude that we are philatelists, a word that sounds slightly risqué but is the correct name for stamp collectors. Philatelists we are not. There is a difference in collecting stamps and accumulating them.

Recently, philatelists had a field day. Bill Gross of Newport Beach, California, was just one stamp shy of having a complete collection of every United States postage stamp issued during the nineteenth century, a total of about 300 rare stamps. The missing treasure was a small, 1868 blue-hued one-cent stamp bearing the image of the first Postmaster General, Benjamin Franklin. Only two are known to exist. Donald Sundman, of Camden, New Jersey, owned one.

Donald and Bill worked out a swap. Bill traded a block of four twenty-four-cent "Inverted Jenny" stamps for Donald's rare one-cent stamp. The "Inverted Jenny" stamps are an equally rare misprinted issue depicting an upside-down airplane. Both the one-cent stamp and the block of four were valued at three million dollars. Talk about postal rate inflation!

Several years ago, my sister-in-law needed to mail a package. She was a school guidance counselor in rural North Carolina. She could only go to the small country post office after work. On Monday, the post office was closed. The sign on the door, crudely written, read, "Closed—We Are Bush Hogging." She tried again Tuesday afternoon, only to find a new sign. It read, "Closed—We Are Dipping Our Dogs." Undaunted, she returned on Wednesday. The post office was open. She took her place in line behind a man in overalls. As he stepped to the window, he said, "I wanna buy some of them stamps y'all have already done licked." Philatelists take note: a rare stamp indeed.

When I think about it, thirty-seven cents, or whatever the new rate will be, is a small price to pay to send a birthday card from South Carolina to a grandchild in Michigan.

The inscription on the New York City Post Office was adapted from the Greek historian, Herodotus. "Neither snow, nor rain, nor heat, nor gloom of night stays these couriers from the swift completion of their appointed rounds." No mention of bush hogging, dog dipping, or lunch breaks.

"Here they are. I've never heard of them," she said.

Bless Your Heart

When I shop at the grocery store, I jockey for position in the shortest checkout line. Inevitably, the line I choose, though it may be the shortest, is also the slowest. So I wait, sometimes conversing with folks I know, sometimes glancing at the tabloid headlines. For example, just last week I learned that Britney Spears is on the verge of her second divorce in two years.

The lady who was in line ahead of me commented on the young celebrity's marital history. "Bless her heart," the woman said.

"Yes, bless her heart!" the clerk replied.

I wondered, "Bless her heart?" What exactly does that mean?

Southerners use the expression for several reasons. It can be used to soften or even disguise an insult. As long as the degrading comment is prefaced with "Bless her heart" or "Bless his heart," the insult may seem sympathetic. "Bless his heart. He's just not playing with a full deck." Or, "Bless her heart, I'm sure she thinks that dress looks good on her."

The phrase can be used to buffer gossip, somehow making it seem more palatable. "You know, even though they've been married only seven months, bless their hearts, their baby still had a head full of hair!"

As long as the person's heart is blessed, the rumor comes across as less severe.

"Bless his heart. You know he does try to control his drinking problem."

A friend announced to a church group, "My dentist told me I have to have a root canal and a crown on this broken tooth."

As if they had rehearsed for a choral anthem, the group responded in unison, "Bless your heart!" It was a genuine expression of sympathy by caring people who could identify with the plight of the sufferer.

In its purest form, "Bless your heart" is a simple prayer.

The phrase "Bless your heart" seems to be most creatively used by a person from the South when speaking to or about a person from the North.

When I was a freshman in college, there was a fellow who, bless his heart, was from New York. He was a fine-looking young man except, bless his heart, he couldn't do a thing with his hair. He had never even heard of a cowlick though, bless his heart, he carried a classic one on the back of his head.

He was smart enough. He did fine in languages in the classroom, both with English and with Spanish, but, bless his heart, he could not understand ordinary conversation. Y'all was a new word to him. He constantly said, "You guys."

Simple sentences were a mystery. I once asked him to cut off the light, and, bless his heart, he started looking around for a pair of scissors or a knife.

He drove a nice, late model automobile. I did not have a car, but I would sometimes borrow one from my uncle. When I asked the New Yorker if he could carry me to my uncle's place of business, bless his heart, he thought I was expecting him to give me a piggyback ride. Bless his heart, he didn't even know what piggyback meant.

He had no hesitation about cursing, though he didn't know a thing about cussing. Bless his heart, he thought nothing of taking the Lord's name in vain. My mama would have washed his mouth out with soap. Though I had grown up on a lumberyard, my mama had tried to teach me not to swear. Instead, I would say, "I swanee." Mama, bless her heart, was not even sure if I should say that.

Other than country music and NASCAR, I suppose there is currently no institution that

takes the ways of the South into the North quite like a company that was started in Lebanon, Tennessee. Not since General Robert E. Lee crossed the Mason-Dixon Line to fight the Yankees at Gettysburg has there been a Southern invasion quite like the peaceful one that Cracker Barrel restaurants have pulled off. From the rocking chairs on the front porch, to the Southern Gospel CDs displayed on spinning racks in the store, to the country cooking in the kitchen, Cracker Barrel can make a displaced soul from Dixie feel right at home.

Several years ago, Clare and I were driving to Michigan to visit our son, bless his heart. We stopped at a Cracker Barrel in central Ohio tucked in between two of the hundreds of large cornfields. Everything about the place made us feel right at home, except for the waitress, bless her heart.

I knew we were in trouble when she said, "What can I bring you guys to drink?"

I perused the familiar menu, and we ordered breakfast. Scrambled eggs, bacon, sausage, buttermilk biscuits with sawmill gravy, and grits, all low carb, of course.

"What was that last thing you ordered?" she asked.

"Grits," I said.

"I don't think we have any of that," she said, scratching her head with her pencil.

I thought of all of those Ohio cornfields, stretching as far as the eye could see. We had just driven past miles of corn. So much corn, so little grits.

"Ask them back in the kitchen to fix me a bowl of grits. They'll know what I mean."

Sure enough, she brought grits with breakfast.

"Here they are. I've never heard of them," she said.

"Bless your heart!"

Taking the High Road

Recently Clare and I drove through the mountains. The high mountains will soon be in their full autumn glory. There is no better way to take in the wonder of this season than a road trip along the Blue Ridge Parkway.

The Blue Ridge Parkway was conceived during the Great Depression, a scenic link between the Shenandoah National Park and the Great Smoky Mountains. The project was designed to put unemployed people to work.

The two-lane highway stretches 469 miles across the southern Appalachian Mountains. As the crow flies, the Parkway may be the shortest route between two parks, but certainly not the quickest. With its many ups and downs, twists and turns, and a speed limit that would be the minimum on most highways, driving the Parkway takes time

The Civilian Conservation Corps began construction in 1935 on several sections of the Parkway simultaneously. Contractors were mandated to hire local people whenever possible, giving priority where employment needs were greatest. Almost all work on the Parkway, including the rigorous chore of tunnel digging, was done by hand with very little machinery.

The work was not completely finished until 1987 when the Linn Cove Viaduct around Grandfather Mountain was completed.

Constructing a road usually begins with an engineer. The Parkway began with a landscape architect who wanted to create a roadway that would blend with the natural surroundings, showcasing the panoramic views of the mountains.

Structures along the route utilized modern materials like concrete for bridges, tunnels, and dams. Stonemasons later finished the work with facings of local stone.

The Parkway is a scenic byway with many natural attractions; it is also a cross-section of Appalachian history, preserving some of the oldest Native American and pioneer settlements. Overlook signs and visitor exhibits alert travelers to points of interest.

The Cherokee and the Tutelo tribes were among the earliest inhabitants of the Blue Ridge. Mountain and river names reflect Native American influence.

Surviving examples of early Appalachian pioneer structures are open to the public. For example, Puckett Cabin was the humble abode of Mrs. Orleana Hawks Puckett, a busy mountain midwife of the late nineteenth century.

Along the Parkway are examples of nineteenth-century industrial development. Mabry Mill is one of the most photographed locations along the Parkway. It features a blacksmith shop, wheelwright's shop,

and whiskey still, as well as the old mill.

Traditional crafts and music still thrive in the Blue Ridge Mountains. Along the Parkway in North Carolina are several places to purchase locally made items, and to enjoy good ole mountain music.

I never tire of the drama I witness on the Parkway stage. Emerging from a sleeping bag in Shining Rock Wilderness to a gold and silver sunrise and pausing on Black Balsam Knob to take in a purple and pink sunset both leave an indelible impression, even on a colorblind pastor. Watching white billows moved by the wind cast their shadows across the face of sunlit mountains, following the path of a black anvil cloud flashing lightning as it moves up a distant valley are equally breathtaking.

The Parkway is a stage for all seasons. I awakened in a tent to a gentle snowfall one morning at Crabtree Meadows. One spring day, I parked my truck at an overlook, not to enjoy the view, but because I couldn't see anything! Torrential rain and echoing thunder had stopped me in my tracks. Later, the storm passed, and I was treated to a spectacular rainbow arching from the top of Mount Pisgah down to Looking Glass Rock.

The mountains offer both the comedy and the tragedy of the ancient Greek theatre. Our family was camping near Doughton Park. We arrived late. Clare served our young boys Kentucky Fried Chicken while I pitched the tent by flashlight. I heard snickers in the darkness. I turned the beam of light toward the giggles to discover that we had guests. Joining our young sons at the picnic table was a pair of raccoons, each with the mask of comedy and chicken-stealing on their minds.

One afternoon, I took a

detour on the Parkway. A wild turkey hen and her nine chicks crossed the pavement in front of me. I stopped and waited while the mother hurried her brood to safety. Four roaring motorcycles were coming down the mountain in the other lane. One straggling chick was killed. There is tragedy here as well.

Bull Creek Valley Overlook identifies the last place an American bison was killed in North Carolina. I paused there, just above 3,500 feet, to gaze at a magnificent display of turning leaves. Walking a short distance down a trail, I was surprised to find a skunk curled up inside the hollow base of a shagbark hickory tree. Not wanting to disturb his sleep, I made a quick retreat.

Later, I watched monarch butterflies dance on wild blue asters. I saw a pair of red-tailed hawks catch an updraft, circling high above me.

The Blue Ridge Parkway is a sanctuary—maybe not for the last buffalo or the turkey chick, but for butterflies and the asters they visit, for hickory trees and the skunks they shelter, for soaring hawks, and for me.

To visit the Parkway is to slow down and examine the pace of my life.

It is a place where my soul is restored.

When a Simple Answer Will Do

A physics professor at a large university gave his class a one-question final exam. The question was: Explain how to determine the height of a skyscraper by using a simple barometer.

One particularly bright student responded: There are three ways to determine the height of a skyscraper by using a simple barometer. The answer I believe you are looking for is to measure the barometric pressure at both the top and the bottom of the building. The difference between the two measurements, assuming a uniform temperature, can be used to compute the height of the building by applying the appropriate equation. A second way to determine the height of the skyscraper is to weigh the barometer. Drop it from the top of the building measuring how long it takes to hit the ground. Using the equation for the acceleration of a falling object, and assuming negligible air resistance, the height of the building can be computed.

The student added: There is a third, much easier way, to determine the height of a skyscraper using a simple barometer. Go to the owner of the building and say, "Tell me how high your skyscraper is, and I'll give you a neat barometer."

The student made an A+ on the exam.

There is a wise, old saying: "For every complex problem, there is a simple answer, and it is almost always wrong." But, it is not always true. Sometimes a simple answer will do.

A family was traveling on Interstate 85 between Atlanta and Spartanburg. Somewhere near the state line, a nine-year-old girl leaned across the seat and asked her mother, "Mama, where did I come from?" It was the big birds-and-bees question the mother had been expecting. The mother, who had rehearsed her answer over and over, launched into her long answer. She gave her child an anatomy lesson, detailing the human reproductive system. Once the basic plumbing was discussed, she went into her dissertation on love and marriage, conception, and childbirth. At the end of the long soliloquy, she asked, "Do you have any questions?"

"No, Mama! I mean did I come from Atlanta or Charlotte?"

Sometimes people ask for a bowl of coleslaw, and we give them a truckload of cabbage.

Often a simple answer is better than a long explanation. Military officers are taught to remember the acronym KISS—Keep It Simple, Stupid. KISS is important in every walk of life.

Three college professors arranged a fishing trip in the wilderness of Alaska. They looked forward to wading in pristine streams, casting for salmon. They had engaged a fishing guide to lead their adventure. They flew from Anchorage to the riverside cabin where they were to meet their guide. The plane made a smooth landing on the water and put them out on a dock near the cabin. The temperature was cold, as expected. Arriving at the cabin door, they knocked. No one answered. The smell of wood smoke from a fire inside the cabin beckoned.

The door swung open. They were astonished at the sight before them. The fire was in a wood-burning stove, but the stove was not on the floor. It was suspended with a network of steel wire halfway between the floor and the ceiling. The psychology professor spoke first, "We have hired a sick man to be our guide. Obviously he has a death wish. He has recklessly endangered himself." The physics professor countered, "No, our guide is a brilliant man who understands thermodynamics. He has placed the heat source in the exact center of the cabin so that warmth is distributed evenly throughout." "No," said the religion professor, "this man is deeply devout, although primitive, in his religious beliefs. He has adopted the ancient concept of fire as a symbol of the divine and has elevated it to a place of importance."

About that time the fishing guide entered the cabin. After a few pleasantries, one of the learned men asked, "Can you tell us why your wood stove is situated as it is?"

"Sure can," said the guide. "I just had a whole lot of baling wire and not enough stove pipe."

There are times when the simple answer will do.

The Night I Came of Age in Andrews Field House

On a cold rainy night in November 1959, I hobbled to old Snyder Field at Wofford College. I had just gotten off crutches following an injury in a junior varsity football game. In those days, aspiring high school athletes were admitted free to Wofford football games.

The annual battle between Wofford and Furman was scheduled for Saturday night. I wanted to be there.

I asked Dad if I could take the family station wagon, a blue 1955 Pontiac we had dubbed the Blue Goose. He consented. I went to the Beacon beforehand, a game day ritual even then. By the size of the crowd at John White's dining establishment, I knew the gridiron contest would be well attended.

Parking space at the game was scarce. I left the Blue Goose on a back street and walked across campus to the stadium. The night air was cold, damp, and filled with enthusiastic cheers. I zipped my London Fog jacket up to my neck, shoved my hands in the pockets, and entered the assigned gate, the one behind Andrews Field House, the one designated for scrawny high school athletes.

Under the bright lights of Snyder Field, I found a group of friends on the cinder track behind the goalpost. We huddled against the cold like a covey of quail, not even trying to find a seat. Throughout the game we moved between the concession stand and the chain link fence behind the end zone.

All of the scoring occurred in the first half. Furman kicked a field goal. Wofford completed its first touchdown pass of a mediocre season. The extra point failed. The score at halftime, 6-3, turned out to be the final score.

The second half was a defensive struggle marred by multiple turnovers. Furman mounted a promising drive in the waning moments. Timeouts were taken. Having downed several Coca-Colas, I really needed to find a restroom, but the game was almost over. I didn't want to miss anything. I waited until the clock ticked down to zero. The contest ended near the goal line, both teams caked in mud.

It was that final drive by the Purple Hurricane that got me into trouble.

I desperately needed to find a restroom. I dashed for Andrews Field House. The big doors were open, but the gentlemen's restroom was locked. Frantically, I tried the door to the ladies' room. Mercifully, it opened. I chose the center stall and found blessed relief.

No sooner had my urgency been eased than a more severe agony ensued. I heard voices, women's voices. I was trapped in the middle stall. I raised my feet out of sight, placing one muddy loafer on either side of the door, gripping the handle with all my might.

At fifteen, painfully shy, I liked girls, but only from a distance. Though the oldest of eight children, four of whom were sisters, I knew very little about the opposite sex. The occupants of the ladies' room were not girls. They were women, college women.

I broke into a sweat as I hid in my cubicle. These women were just too close for comfort. Their conversations were all around me, echoing off the white tile walls.

Many of them were in the same desperate condition as I was when the game ended. No small number of them tried the door of the center stall. Concluding that it was out of order, most complained they could not wait much longer. I was grateful the stall door was positioned low enough to prevent a proper lady from crawling beneath the barrier and discovering my secret hiding place.

I wanted to leave, but I could not. I kept thinking, *In a while the crowd will diminish.*

When the coast is clear, I'll make my escape.

I thought that soon I could just walk out unnoticed. But to my horror, I heard a dance band start playing. Oh, no! There was a party going on. I was trapped in the middle stall of the ladies' room.

I waited. For an hour and a half, I waited.

I listened. I learned.

These women were students from Converse College, Winthrop College, Columbia College, and Queens College, to name a few. They talked to each other about fashion and frustration. They talked about the men they were dating, the men they had dated, and the men they wished they could date. Some shared intimate details of their lives.

That November night, I listened anonymously, a silent teenage priest behind a confessional wall. I was unexpectedly enlightened.

After a time, the crush dwindled to only three women, gathered around the lavatories combing hair, adjusting clothing, and freshening makeup.

Time for my escape! I cleared my throat as deeply as a fifteen-year-old could. Chatty voices fell silent. One said in dismay, "Y'all, it can't be!"

I bellowed, "I've been in here long enough. I'm coming out!"

I took off my glasses, stuffed them in my shirt pocket, and pulled my jacket over my head. Hoping against hope I would not be identified, I dashed for the door.

Barely off crutches, I ran through the wet grass in the dark.

Panting, I jumped in the Blue Goose and drove home.

"Why are you late?" Dad asked. I told the truth. He laughed so hard I thought he'd never stop.

"Don't tell anybody," I pleaded.

"I won't," he promised.

Still laughing, he added, "Someday you'll laugh about it, too. Then you'll tell the story."

He was right!

Tim's Miracle

Tim and Diane Timmons have experienced a miracle. These good friends enjoy life on a modest horse farm in the northern part of Spartanburg County. In April of 1999, Tim was riding his mare, Goldie, when she startled, reared, and fell backwards on top of him. Goldie was frightened but unhurt. Tim suffered a dislocated left hip and a broken left arm.

Following orthopedic surgery, Tim's recovery proceeded as expected. In January of 2004, Tim began experiencing pain in his upper left thigh. By August, the pain was persistent and more intense. X-rays revealed no further complications with the previous injury, but there was a new problem. Tim had bone cancer, a slow-growing tumor on the top half of his left femur.

The orthopedic surgeon referred Tim to M. D. Anderson Hospital in Houston. A trip to Texas for a diagnostic evaluation at the world-famous cancer center gave Tim and Diane the hope of a cure.

They learned that the cancer could not be treated with radiation or chemotherapy. The treatment of choice was to remove the affected area of the femur and replace it with a bone from a donor. The surgery could be performed only after a suitable bone, matched according to size and other criteria, had been located. Tim and Diane returned to their horse farm to wait.

The wait was less than a month. The Timmonses received a call in early September. They quickly prepared to return to Houston. I spoke with them on the night before they left for the long drive to Texas. Tim made a special request, "Dr. Kirk, please pray for the family of the donor. You know, in order for me to receive this bone, somebody had to die. There is a family somewhere that is grieving. Please pray for them."

Diane explained to me why Tim was so concerned for the bereaved family of the donor. In May of 1981, Tim's twenty-five-year-old brother Mark died in a senseless attack. The victim of a teenaged assailant, Mark

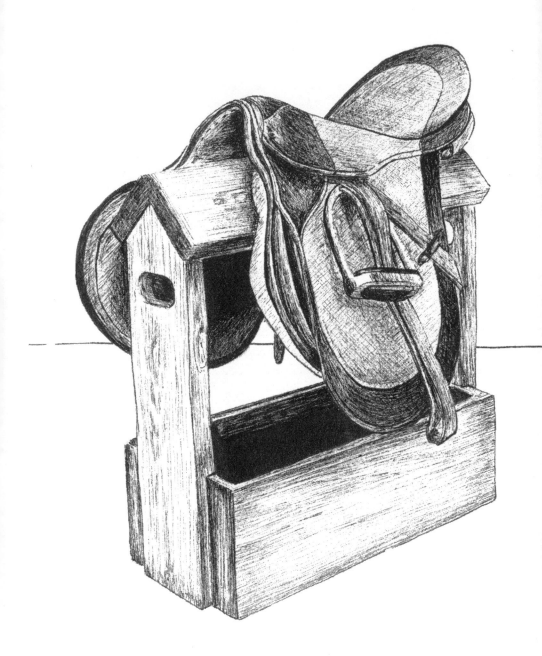

was shot through the heart twice during a robbery. Because of the way Mark died, organ donation was not possible.

Almost exactly a year later, Tim's nineteen-year-old sister, Ann, was in an automobile accident. A freshman at Carson-Newman College, she was rushed to the emergency room at a hospital in Knoxville, Tennessee. Physicians determined that her brain stem had been crushed. Ann survived the night but died early the next morning.

The red heart symbol on her driver's license indicated her desire to be an organ donor. Waiting through the night, her family had the opportunity to carefully consider her request. They consented. Ann's heart, kidneys, and eyes were donated.

In Birmingham, Alabama, a man from Mississippi had been awaiting a heart transplant. A newspaper article carried the story that a suitable heart had been found in Knoxville and had been flown to Birmingham. The transplant was successful.

Friends of the Timmons family, who knew of Ann's death, read the article in the Birmingham newspaper. They put two and two together and sent the newspaper article to Charlotte Timmons, mother of Tim, Mark, and Ann. The families of organ donors and the families of organ recipients usually remain anonymous to each other. The exception is that they can be identified if both parties agree. Charlotte Timmons wanted to meet the man who had received her daughter's heart. Theodis Brown agreed. When Theodis Brown was able to travel, he and his family drove from their home in Mississippi to the Timmons home on the outskirts of Atlanta.

The Browns were houseguests of the Timmons for two days. At a special meal prepared by Charlotte Timmons, Theodis Brown, his wife, and their three little boys sat at the table with the Timmons family. Charlotte asked Theodis to say the blessing. It was a prayer of thanksgiving. A black family from Mississippi and a white family from Georgia shared a meal, brought together because Ann, as a teenager, had made a decision to share her heart. As the Browns prepared to return to Mississippi, the three little boys were invited to each select a miniature horse figurine from Ann's collection. The tiny horses were mementoes of their visit and symbols of their new friendship.

The Timmons are thankful every day for the miracle of life. It is a miracle they have experienced from both sides. When it comes to organ donation, giving and receiving are equally blessed.

Remembering Dirt Roads

The street where our family lived when I was a boy was not a street at all. It was a dirt road. It ran from Mr. Taylor's dairy farm past Mr. Smith's cornfield to the shanty of a mysterious woman I was pretty sure was a witch. She had a big, black cast-iron pot in her yard where she boiled something, maybe curious boys.

The dirt road in front of our home was a trail to adventure. Toward the east, it became a paved road near a natural gas transfer station, a place surrounded by a chain link fence with ominous signs warning KEEP OUT. East was the direction to Tommy Wilson's East End Market and Community Cash grocery store. It was the route I took on my bicycle to go to Monday night scout meetings.

Toward the west, the dirt road led to a path through the woods, over a creek to Dead Horse Canyon, a deep gully that was a marvelous playground.

Beyond the path to the gully, the dirt road went to the witch's shack. The old lady probably was not a witch at all, but she was at least an eccentric recluse. Rarely did I go that far down the road. I went all the way to the end when Gordon Coley dared me and promised me half of a Hershey Bar if I would. On that occasion, I heard a shotgun blast. Whether I was the target or not, I can't say. I ran all the way home. That was the last time I ventured that far.

Dirt roads hold a special charm. I remember the sadness I felt when our road was paved with asphalt. From then on, it was a street, no longer a road.

Recently, on a bright Saturday morning, master photographer Mark Olencki and I traveled to a farm above Highway 11 to visit a fascinating couple. According to James Cooley, who grows excellent peaches and strawberries, these folks own the best-looking team of mules anywhere around. We needed photographs of mules for the cover of this book.

Mark spotted a diamond-shaped Mule Crossing sign. I turned my pickup truck onto a dirt road. We stopped to open a heavy steel gate, carefully locking it behind us. The twin tracks of the lane cut through a cow pasture, followed the curve of a hill down to a soggy bottom, and climbed a slope beyond. Cresting the second rise, we saw the farmhouse in the distance. The dirt road curved to the right, then back to the left past a stately barn.

As the truck neared the house, three dogs announced our arrival: a German shepherd, a Scottish collie, and an English bulldog. Guinea hens scurried across the yard. A handsome rooster of no distinguishable nationality strutted near an old well.

The mules were soon ready for pictures. Mark took a zillion shots, not just of the mules. Though I have "a face for radio," he also took a few of me. Through the lens of his high-tech digital camera, Mark went back in time, taking pictures of the old buildings, of turkeys, of horses, and of the charming house.

After the photo shoot, we were invited into the vintage farmhouse. The earliest part of the structure, a log cabin, was built in 1836. The home now features several additions, including a kitchen and a bathroom with indoor plumbing. We sat by a warm fire in the front room, swapping stories.

As we made our departure, the bulldog was on the porch, chewing the leg bone of a deer. We said our goodbyes and made our way back up the dirt road. I commented to Mark, "I don't think these people are in any danger of burglars."

"Probably not," Mark agreed. "Anybody with bad intentions would have to unlock the gate and make their way through the cow pasture with all of its hazards. When they finally got to the house, they would be greeted by an international assortment of barking dogs and probably a shotgun."

I said, "We'd all be better off if there were more dirt roads."

Too many dirt roads have been paved. Dirt roads slow us down to a more reasonable pace. Dirt roads teach us patience. Walking to the school bus, to the mailbox, or to the store took more time, but provided good exercise. Dirt roads bespeak a different set of values, a quality of character that's worth preserving.

Biographies

Kirk H. Neely is senior pastor of Morningside Baptist Church in Spartanburg, South Carolina. He holds a doctor of ministry degree in pastoral counseling and psychology of religion from The Southern Baptist Theological Seminary. Neely has been a pastor and counselor for over forty years. He is the author of *Comfort & Joy: Nine Stories for Christmas* (Hub City Writers Project, 2006) and *When Grief Comes: Strength for Today, Hope for Tomorrow* (Baker Publishing Group, 2007).

Emory Cash is a native of Spartanburg, South Carolina, where he attended Spartanburg High School. He continued his education at Anderson University, earning a bachelor of arts degree with a concentration in painting and drawing. He and his wife, Tara, live in Greenville, South Carolina, where he works as an art director for a marketing firm.

 The Hub City Writers Project is a non-profit organization whose mission is to foster a sense of community through the literary arts. We do this by publishing books from and about our community; encouraging, mentoring, and advancing the careers of local writers; and seeking to make Spartanburg a center for the literary arts.

Our metaphor of organization purposely looks backward to the nineteenth century when Spartanburg was known as the "hub city," a place where railroads converged and departed.

At the beginning of the twenty-first century, Spartanburg has become a literary hub of South Carolina with an active and nationally celebrated core group of poets, fiction writers, and essayists. We celebrate these writers—and the ones not yet discovered—as one of our community's greatest assets. William R. Ferris, former director of the Center for the Study of Southern Cultures, says of the emerging South, "Our culture is our greatest resource. We can shape an economic base ... And it won't be an investment that will disappear."

Our Titles

Hub City Anthology • John Lane, Betsy Wakefield Teter, editors
Hub City Music Makers • Peter Cooper
Hub City Christmas • John Lane, Betsy Wakefield Teter, editors
New Southern Harmonies • Rosa Shand, Scott Gould,
Deno Trakas, George Singleton
The Best of Radio Free Bubba • Meg Barnhouse, Pat Jobe, Kim Taylor, Gary Phillips
Family Trees: The Peach Culture of the Piedmont • Mike Corbin
Seeing Spartanburg: A History in Images • Philip Racine
The Seasons of Harold Hatcher • Mike Hembree
The Lawson's Fork: Headwaters to Confluence • David Taylor, Gary Henderson
Hub City Anthology 2 • Betsy Wakefield Teter, editor
Inheritance • Janette Turner Hospital, editor
In Morgan's Shadow • The Hub City Writers Project
Eureka Mill • Ron Rash
The Place I Live • The Children of Spartanburg County
Textile Town • The Hub City Writers Project
Come to the Cow Pens! • Christine Swager
Noticing Eden • Marjory Heath Wentworth
Noble Trees of the South Carolina Upstate • Mark Dennis, John Lane, Mark Olencki
Literary South Carolina • Edwin Epps
Magical Places • Marion Peter Holt
When the Soldiers Came to Town • Susan Turpin, Carolyn Creal,
Ron Crawley, James Crocker
Twenty: South Carolina Poetry Fellows • Kwame Dawes, editor
The Return of Radio Free Bubba • Meg Barnhouse, Pat Jobe, Kim Taylor
Hidden Voices • Kristofer Neely, editor
Wofford: Shining with Untarnished Honor • Doyle Boggs, JoAnn Mitchell Brasington, Phillip Stone, editors
South of Main • Beatrice Hill, Brenda Lee, compilers
Cottonwood Trail • Thomas Webster, G.R. Davis, Jr., Peter L. Schmunk
Courageous Kate • Sheila Ingle
Comfort & Joy • Kirk H. Neely, June Neely Kern
Common Ties • Katherine Davis Cann
Spartanburg Revisited: A Second Look at the Photographs of Alfred & Bob Willis
• Carroll Foster, Mark Olencki
This Threshold • Scott Neely, editor
Still Home • Rachel Harkai, editor
Best of the Kudzu Telegraph • John Lane
Stars Fell on Spartanburg • Jeremy L.C. Jones and Betsy Wakefield Teter, editors
Ask Mr. Smartypants • Lane Filler
Two South Carolina Plays • Jon Tuttle
Through the Pale Door • Brian Ray